ENVIRONMENT QUIZ BOOK

Find Answers to all your Queries

I0642456

Manasvi Vohra

V&S PUBLISHERS

Published by:

V&S PUBLISHERS

F-2/16, Ansari Road, Daryaganj, New Delhi-110002
011-23240026, 011-23240027 • *Fax:* 011-23240028
Email: info@vspublishers.com • *Website:* www.vspublishers.com

Branch : Hyderabad
5-1-707/1, Brij Bhawan (Beside Central Bank of India Lane)
Bank Street, Koti, Hyderabad - 500 095
040-24737290
E-mail: vspublishershyd@gmail.com

Follow us on:

For any assistance sms **VSPUB** to **56161**

All books available at **www.vspublishers.com**

Publisher's Note

We all know the importance of environment and the environmental factors that influence our lives, in fact our very existence. Today, people have become more and more conscious towards a healthier environment formulating policies, programmes and means to improve and safeguard the environment from various detrimental factors, such as pollution, global warming, deforestation, natural and man-made disasters, etc.

The **Environment Quiz Book** serves as a comprehensive and complete package containing exhaustive information about the environment, the factors influencing it, the salient inventions and discoveries relating to the ever-changing environment and answers to the innumerable questions that arise in our minds, particularly the young minds of school and college going students. The book has been divided into separate sections with simple and intersasting Questions, Fill in the Blanks, Multiple Choice Questions, True & False, Word Search & Crossword – all with *Soutions* to satisfy the readers' curiosities and enrich their knowledge and awareness towards the environment.

Basically, the book aims to arouse the readers' interests towards the many different and unique environmental phenomena occuring always all around us and also to enlighten the readers towards a *healthier, cleaner and safer environment.*

QUESTIONS

&

ANSWERS

Questions & Answers

Q-1. What is the natural surroundings in which an organism lives called?
Ans. The natural surroundings in which an organism lives is called its habitat.

Q-2. When is the Earth Environment Day celebrated?
Ans. June 5.

Q-3. What is air made up of?
Ans. Air is made up of mainly oxygen (O) and nitrogen (N), small amounts of water vapour, argon, and carbon dioxide, along with small traces of other gases.

Q-4. When is the Earth Day celebrated?
Ans. April 22.

Q-5. What does recycling mean?
Ans. Recycling means to extract materials from waste and reuse it.

Q-6. What are the three R's of recycling?
Ans. The three R's of recycling are reduce, reuse and recycle.

Q-7. What is deforestation?
Ans. The permanent cutting or destruction of forests is called deforestation.

Q-8. How much of the earth is covered by water?
Ans. Approximately 70% of the earth is covered by water.

Q-9. When is the World Water Day celebrated?
Ans. March 22.

RADIOACTIVITY

Q-10. What is an isotope?
Ans. When an element exists in more than one form with different mass numbers (due to varying number of neutrons), it is said to have isotopes. For example, Carbon-12, Carbon-13 and Carbon-14 are isotopes of carbon.

Q-11. What is radioactivity?
Ans. Radioactivity is the emission of high energy from unstable atoms. The nuclei of these atoms break down and release energy. It may be natural or artificial.

Q-12. What are the components of radiation produced during radioactivity?
Ans. Alpha rays, beta rays and gamma rays are the chief components of radiation produced during radioactivity.

Q-13. Who discovered the phenomenon of natural radio-activity?
Ans. Natural radioactivity was first discovered by a French scientist, Henri Becquerel in 1896.

Q-14. Name one beneficial and one harmful use of radioactivity in modern world.
Ans. Radioactivity is used in cancer treatments. However, the principle of radioactivity is also used in the atomic bombs.

Q-15. When did the first atomic bomb explosion take place?
Ans. The first atomic bomb explosion took place in the Japanese city of Hiroshima on August 6, 1945 during World War II.

OZONE LAYER

Q-16. What is the ozone layer?
Ans. Ozone layer is a layer of ozone molecules in the stratosphere which protects the earth from the harmful ultraviolet rays of the sun.

Mushroom cloud of atomic bomb explosion

Q-17. What is ozone hole?
Ans. An ozone hole is a geographical area above the Antarctic region where the concentration of ozone molecules has decreased, thus thinning the ozone layer.

Q-18. What causes the depletion of ozone molecules?
Ans. Production of certain man-made chlorine compounds like chlorofluorocarbons (CFCs), methyl chloroform and carbon tetrachloride cause the depletion of ozone molecules.

Q-19. When was the hole in the ozone layer first discovered?
Ans. The hole in the ozone layer was first discovered in 1985 by British scientists Joseph Farman, Brian Gardiner and Jonathan Shanklin.

Q-20. What is Montreal Protocol?
Ans. The Montreal Protocol on Substances that Deplete the Ozone Layer is an international agreement signed in 1987 and ratified by most countries towards phasing out the production of substances that cause the depletion of the ozone layer.

Q-21. When did India sign the Montreal Protocol?
Ans. India signed the Montreal Protocol in 1992.

GLOBAL WARMING

Q-22. What are greenhouse gases?
Ans. Greenhouse gases are gases which trap the heat in the atmosphere, e.g. carbon dioxide.

Q-23. What is global warming?
Ans. Global warming is the steady increase of the earth's temperature.

Q-24. What are the man-made causes of global warming?
Ans. The greenhouse gases produced by human activities and rampant deforestation are the two main man-made causes of global warming.

Q-25. What are the effects of global warming?
Ans. Extreme weather, melting of glaciers, increase in the sea level and climate changes are some of the effects of global warming.

Q-26. What is Kyoto Protocol?
Ans. Kyoto Protocol is an international agreement aimed at controlling the emission of greenhouse gases.

Q-27. When and where was Kyoto Protocol signed?
Ans. Kyoto Protocol was first adopted in 1997 in Kyoto, Japan.

Q-28. According to the Indian constitution, it is the state's and citizens' responsibility to protect the environment. Is it true or false?
Ans. Yes, it is true.

POPULATION

Q-29. Which is the most populated country in the world?
Ans. China.

Q-30. How is population density of a place measured?
Ans. The population density of a place is measured in terms of population per unit area.

Q-31. Which country or state has the highest population density in the world?
Ans. Monaco.

Q-32. State two effects of overpopulation on the earth.
Ans. Depletion of natural resources and destruction of ecosystems are the two effects caused by overpopulation on the earth.

EXTINCTION

Q-33. What do you mean by extinction of a species?
Ans. A species becomes extinct when all the members of the species die out.

Q-34. State any two causes of animal extinction.
Ans. Poaching (or illegal hunting) and habitat destruction are two causes of animal extinction.

Q-35. Name any two animals that have become extinct in recent times.
Ans. Tasmanian wolf and Japanese sea lion are among animals that have become extinct in recent times.

Q-36. Name one bird that has become extinct.
Ans. Dodo is a bird species that became extinct before the 18th century.

Dodo

Q-37. Name any two critically endangered species in India.
Ans. Long-billed vulture and gharial are among the two critically endangered species in India.

ECOSYSTEM

Q-38. What is an ecosystem?
Ans. An ecosystem is an ecological community consisting of biotic, abiotic as well as components which interact with each other and function as a single unit.

Q-39. List the three main types of ecosystems.
Ans. The three main types of ecosystems are:

– Freshwater ecosystem
– Terrestrial ecosystem
– Ocean ecosystem

Q-40. What is a terrestrial ecosystem?
Ans. A terrestrial ecosystem is an ecosystem formed on a landform.

Q-41. Which categories can a terrestrial ecosystem be divided into?
Ans. A terrestrial ecosystem can be divided into these main categories: tropical rainforest, taiga, desert, savanna and tundra.

Q-42. Give one example of a tropical rainforest ecosystem.
Ans. Amazon rainforest is an example of a tropical rainforest ecosystem.

Q-43. Give one characteristic of a savanna.
Ans. A savanna is a grassland ecosystem characterised by wide spaces between trees and seasonal rainfall.

Q-44. What is taiga?
Ans. Taiga is a belt of coniferous forests that is usually found in the northern hemisphere in difficult weather conditions.

Savanna grasslands

Q-45. Give one example of a desert ecosystem.
Ans. The Sahara desert in Africa is an example of a desert ecosystem.

Q-46. Give two characteristics of a tundra ecosystem.
Ans. Extremely cold climate and low biodiversity are two characteristics of a tundra ecosystem.

CONSERVATION

Q-47. What is conservation?
Ans. Conservation is the act of preservation, protection and restoration of the natural environment.

Q-48. What does UNEP stand for?
Ans. UNEP stands for the United Nations Environment Programme.

Q-49. What is the role of UNEP?
Ans. UNEP helps and encourages countries to formulate and implement environment-related policies. It coordinates all environmental activities of the United Nations (UN).

Q-50. When was UNEP established?
Ans. UNEP was established in June 1972 in Nairobi, Kenya.

Q-51. What is ecology?
Ans. Ecology is the study of living beings and their relationship with their surroundings.

Q-52. Who coined the word 'ecology'?
Ans. The word 'ecology' was coined by Ernst Haeckel in 1866.

Q-53. What are the four important components of an ecosystem?
Ans. The four important components of an ecosystem are: environment, producers, consumers and decomposers.

Q-54. Who are the producers in an ecosystem?
Ans. Green plants/trees are the producers in an ecosystem.

Q-55. Who are the consumers in an ecosystem?
Ans. Animals are the consumers in an ecosystem.

Q-56. Who are the decomposers in an ecosystem?
Ans. Bacteria, fungi and insects act as decomposers in an ecosystem.

Q-57. What is the role of decomposers in an ecosystem?
Ans. Decomposers consume dead plants and animals, breaking them down into basic components.

Q-58. Based on their eating habits, how many groups can animals be categorised into?
Ans. Based on their eating habits, animals can be *herbivorous*, *carnivorous* and *omnivorous*.

Q-59. What are herbivorous animals?
Ans. Herbivorous animals are those that eat only plants and vegetation. For example, cows, rabbits, etc.

Q-60. What are carnivorous animals?
Ans. Carnivorous animals are those that eat other animals. For example, tiger, lion, etc.

Q-61. What are omnivorous animals?
Ans. Omnivorous animals are those that can eat both plants and other animals. Humans are omnivores.

Q-62. What is a food chain?
Ans. A food chain is an ecological sequence in which living organisms are shown to be dependent on each other for sustenance. For example, a deer eats grass, and a deer is eaten by a lion, and so on.

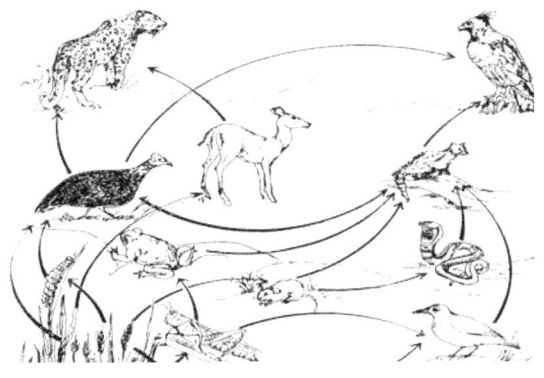

A food chain

Q-63. What is a food web?
Ans. In an ecosystem, all animals and plants are interconnected based on their feeding habits and requirements, in such a way that every living organism is dependent on another for sustenance. This complex series of several overlapping food chains is called a food web.

Q-64. Which is the first element of any food chain?
Ans. Green plants are the first element of all food chains.

Q-65. Can plants be carnivores too?
Ans. Yes, some plants are known to be carnivorous.

Q-66. Give two examples of carnivorous plants?
Ans. Venus Flytrap and pitcher.

Q-67. What are saprophytes?
Ans. Saprophytes are living organisms that consume dead and decayed organic matter.

Q-68. Give two examples of saprophytes.
Ans. Bacteria and fungi are two types of saprophytes.

Q-69. What are parasites?
Ans. Parasites are those living organisms that live on the bodies of other living organisms.

Q-70. What are the two types of parasites?
Ans. The two types of parasites are – endoparasites and ectoparasites.

Q-71. What are endoparasites?
Ans. Endoparasites are those that live inside the body of the host organism.

Q-72. Give one example of an endoparasite.
Ans. Tapeworms.

Q-73. What are ectoparasites?
Ans. Ectoparasites are parasites that live on the exterior parts of the host organism's body.

Q-74. Give one example of an ectoparasite.
Ans. Fleas.

Q-75. What is photosynthesis?
Ans. Photosynthesis is the process through which plants create their own food with the help of sunlight.

Q-76. What are the biotic components of an ecosystem?
Ans. The living elements of an ecosystem constitute its biotic components.

Q-77. What are the abiotic elements of an ecosystem?
Ans. The non-living elements of an ecosystem constitute its abiotic components.

Q-78. Name one biotic component of an ecosystem.
Ans. Plants and animals are biotic components of an ecosystem.

Q-79. Name one abiotic component of an ecosystem.
Ans. Environment is an abiotic component of an ecosystem.

Q-80. Where does the earth's atmosphere begin?
Ans. The earth's atmosphere begins right from its surface.

Q-81. What happens to the density of the atmosphere as its distance from the earth's surface increases?
Ans. The density of the atmosphere decreases in relation to its distance from the earth's surface.

Q-82. Who are ethologists?
Ans. Scientists who study the behaviour of wild animals are called the ethologists.

Q-83. Define terricolous animals.
Ans. Animals that live in the soil are called terricolous animals.

Q-84. Give an example of a terricolous animal.
Ans. An earthworm.

Q-85. What are arboreal animals?
Ans. Arboreal animals are those that live on trees.

Q-86. Name one arboreal animal.
Ans. Monkey.

Q-87. What is a biome?
Ans. A biome is a major group of flora and fauna found in a region shaped by common patterns of climate.

Q-88. Give two examples of biomes.
Ans. Desert biomes and forest biomes.

Q-89. What is the difference between biomes and ecosystem?
Ans. Biomes are larger than ecosystems; one biome may contain several ecosystems.

Q-90. What do you understand by biodegradation?
Ans. The natural breakdown of substances into simpler forms that can be used by other organisms of the biosphere is called biodegradation.

Q-91. Are all substances biodegradable?
Ans. No, all substances are not biodegradable.

Q-92. What is adaptation?
Ans. Adaptation is the process by which an organism changes itself to survive in a changing environment.

Q-93. What are the two common types of adaptations?
Ans. Adaptations can be individual or an entire species can undergo adaptation.

Q-94. How is individual adaptation different from group adaptation?
Ans. Individual adaptation takes place during an organism's lifetime, while group adaptation happens more gradually over a long period of time.

Q-95. What happens to living things that fail to adapt to a new environment?
Ans. Living things that fail to adapt to a new environment are unable to survive for long, and become extinct.

Q-96. Who is Charles Darwin?
Ans. Charles Darwin was an English naturalist who gave the theory of evolution.

Questions & Answers

Charles Darwin

Q-97. What is evolution?
Ans. Evolution is the change in the hereditary characteristics that successive generations of a species develop or display over a long period of time.

Q-98. What is anthropology?
Ans. Anthropology is the scientific study of the origin of the human beings and their physical, social and cultural development over the ages.

Q-99. What is camouflage?
Ans. Camouflage is a defence technique used by certain animals by which they change their appearance to match their surroundings so as to hide from predators.

Q-100. What are predators?
Ans. Predators are animals that prey on other animals.

Q-101. What is hibernation?
Ans. In order to survive harsh winters, certain animals go into hiding during the whole season. This phenomenon is called hibernation.

Q-102. Name any two animals that hibernate.
Ans. Frogs and some species of bears hibernate during winter.

Q-103. What is aestivation?
Ans. Aestivation is the process in which certain animals go in hiding during dry summers.

Q-104. Name any two animals who aestivate.
Ans. Crocodiles and some species of land snails aestivate during summer.

Q-105. What are benthos?
Ans. Organisms that live at the bottom of a sea or a lake are called benthos.

Q-106. What are planktons?
Ans. Planktons are plants and animals found drifting under water. They are common source of food for water animals.

Q-107. Who is called the 'father of evolution'?
Ans. Charles Darwin.

Q-108. How many structural layers does the earth have?
Ans. The earth has three major structural layers.

Q-109. Name the three structural layers of the earth.
Ans. Crust, Mantle and Core.

Q-110. Define crust.
Ans. Crust is the outermost layer of the earth's surface.

Q-111. What does the earth's crust consist of?
Ans. The earth's crust consists of continents and ocean basins.

Q-112. How thick is the earth's crust?
Ans. The earth's crust is 35–70 km thick in the continents and 5–10 km thick in the ocean basins.

Q-113. What is the earth's crust composed of?
Ans. The earth's crust is mostly composed of alumina-silicates.

Questions & Answers

Q-114. What is mantle?
Ans. Mantle is the second structural layer of the earth.

Q-115. What is earth's mantle composed of?
Ans. The earth's mantle is mostly composed of ferro-magnesium silicates.

Q-116. How thick is the earth's mantle?
Ans. The earth's mantle is about 2900 km thick.

Q-117. How many layers is the earth's mantle divided into?

Ans. The earth's mantle is divided into two layers – upper mantle and lower mantle.

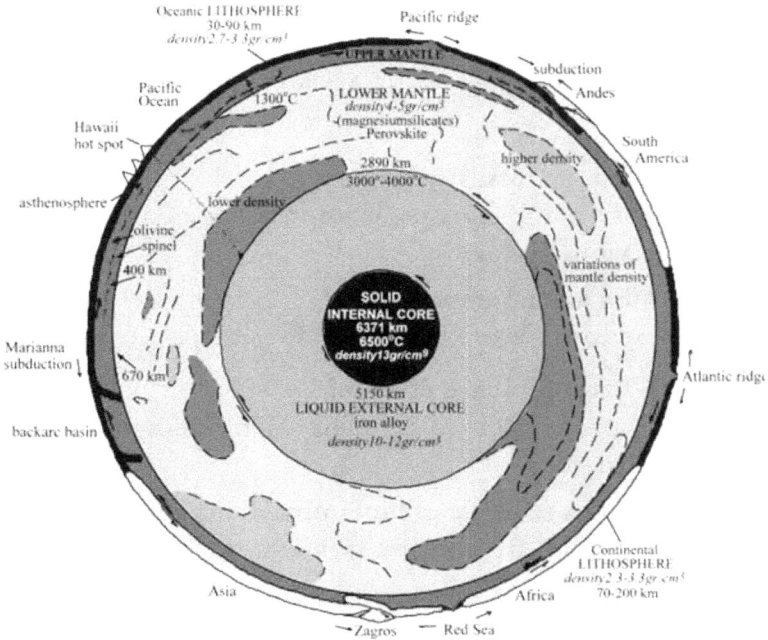

A diagram showing different structural layers of earth

Q-118. What is the earth's core?
Ans. The core is the last structural layer of the earth.

Q-119. How many layers is the earth's core divided into?
Ans. The earth's core is further divided into inner core and outer core.

Q-120. How thick is the earth's core?
Ans. The outer core of the earth is about 2300 km thick and the inner core is around 1200 km thick.

Q-121. What is the outer core of the earth composed of?
Ans. The outer core of the earth is mainly composed of a nickel-iron alloy.

Q-122. What is the inner core of the earth composed of?
Ans. Iron.

Q-123. Which structural layer of the earth controls its magnetic field?
Ans. The outer core of the earth is believed to control its magnetic field.

Q-124. What are fossils?
Ans. Fossils are the remains or impressions of an organism from a previous geologic age.

Q-125. Who are palaeontologists?
Ans. The scientists who study fossils are called palaeontologists.

Q-126. What is bioluminescence?
Ans. The production of light by living beings is called bioluminescence.

Q-127. Give an example of bioluminescence in animals.
Ans. Glow-worms are common examples of bioluminescence.

Q-128. What is the purpose of bioluminescence?
Ans. Bioluminescence is used by living beings for communication, camouflage or to lure their prey.

Q-129. Based on their anatomy, what are the two classes of animals?
Ans. Vertebrates and Invertebrates.

Q-130. What are vertebrates?
Ans. Vertebrates are a class of animals that have spinal columns or backbones.

Q-131. What are invertebrates?
Ans. Invertebrates are a class of animals that don't have spinal columns or backbones.

Q-132. How many types of vertebrates are there?
Ans. Vertebrates are of five types – mammals, birds, fish, reptiles and amphibians.

Q-133. Name two types of animals that are invertebrates.
Ans. Insects and spiders.

Q-134. What are mammals?
Ans. Mammals are warm-blooded vertebrates. They usually give birth to young ones. They mostly have fur or hair on their skin.

Q-135. Give two examples of mammals.
Ans. Dogs and human beings.

Q-136. State two characteristics of birds.
Ans. Birds have feathers and they lay eggs.

Q-137. Are bats birds? Why or why not?
Ans. Bats are mammals, not birds. They do not lay eggs.

Q-138. What is ecological climax?
Ans. When a community reaches a condition of stability, it is called ecological climax.

Q-139. What are reptiles?
Ans. Reptiles are cold-blooded animals with scaly skin.

Q-140. State two examples of reptiles.
Ans. Lizards and crocodiles.

Q-141. What are amphibians?
Ans. Amphibians are animals that can live on both land and water.

Q-142. Give one example of amphibians.
Ans. Frogs.

Q-143. What are arthropods?
Ans. Arthropods are animals that have more than four legs and have an external skeleton.

Q-144. What are cannibals?
Ans. Cannibals are animals that feed on their own species.

Q-145. What are natural resources?
Ans. Natural resources are resources that we get from nature.

Q-146. How can natural resources be classified?
Ans. Natural resources can be classified into inexhaustible, renewable and non-renewable resources.

Q-147. What are inexhaustible natural resources?
Ans. Those natural resources which cannot be exhausted by consumption are called inexhaustible natural resources. For example, air and sunlight are inexhaustible resources.

Q-148. What are renewable resources?
Ans. Renewable resources are those which are naturally replenished after consumption by man, for example water, wood, etc.

Q-149. What are non-renewable resources?
Ans. Non-renewable resources are those that cannot be replenished if consumed entirely, for example, certain metals.

Q-150. What are metals?
Ans. Metals are solid substances found in nature which are ductile, malleable and good conductors of heat and electricity.

Q-151. Name any two metals that are commonly used in jewellery-making?
Ans. Gold and silver.

Q-152. Which is the biggest gold mine in the world?
Ans. The Grasberg mine in Indonesia.

Q-153. What is the main source of energy for the earth?
Ans. Sunlight.

Q-154. Which are the most common sources of energy used by human beings?
Ans. Coal, petroleum and natural gas.

Q-155. What is wind power?
Ans. The mechanical or electrical energy produced with the help of the movement of wind is called the wind power.

Q-156. What are the common derivatives of petroleum?
Ans. Kerosene, diesel, gasoline, etc.

Q-157. What is humidity?
Ans. Water vapour present in the air is called humidity.

Q-158. What is climate?
Ans. Climate is the general pattern of a particular place's weather over the course of an entire year.

Q-159. What is weather?
Ans. Weather is the daily changes in the atmospheric conditions of a place.

Q-160. Which elements is the universe made up of?
Ans. The universe is mostly made up of hydrogen (H) and Helium (He).

Q-161. Which is the rarest naturally occurring element found in the earth's crust?
Ans. Astatine.

Q-162. What are edaphic factors?
Ans. The factors of an environment that are determined by the soil are called edaphic factors.

Q-163. What are diurnal animals?
Ans. Diurnal animals are those which are active only during the day time.

Q-164. What are nocturnal animals?
Ans. Nocturnal animals are those which are active only during the night time.

Q-165. What is a fertilizer?
Ans. A fertilizer is any substance which is added to the soil to provide nutrients.

Q-166. Name any two natural fertilizers.
Ans. Manure and compost.

Q-167. What is manure?
Ans. Faeces and excreta of animals are called manure.

Q-168. What is compost?
Ans. Decayed plant material used as a fertilizer is called compost.

Q-169. Name any two chemical fertilizers.
Ans. Ammonia and urea.

Q-170. What is carbon cycle?
Ans. Carbon cycle is the circulation of carbon atoms in nature.

Q-171. Define pest.
Ans. Pests are living organisms that can harm other living beings.

Q-172. What are pesticides?
Ans. Chemicals used to kill pests are called pesticides.

Q-173. What is environmental monitoring?
Ans. It is the periodic measurement of environmental changes happening around the world.

Questions & Answers

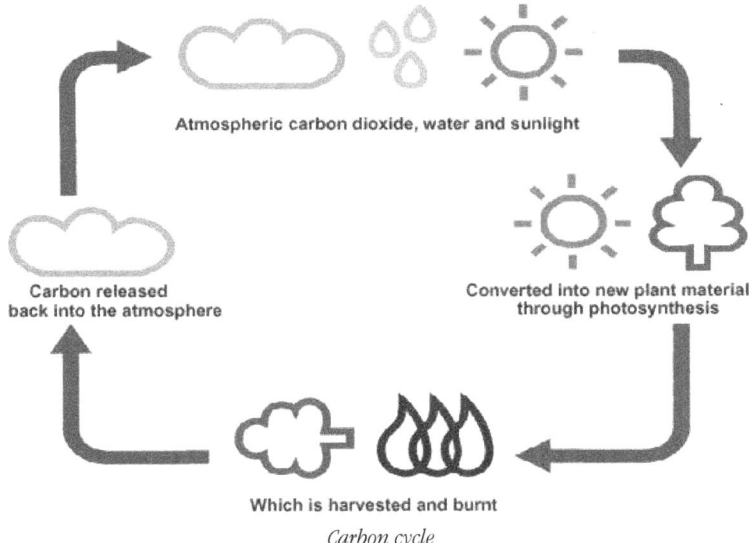

Atmospheric carbon dioxide, water and sunlight

Carbon released back into the atmosphere

Converted into new plant material through photosynthesis

Which is harvested and burnt

Carbon cycle

Q-174. What is nitrogen cycle?
Ans. It is the continuous circulation of atmospheric nitrogen among plants, soil, animals and then back to the atmosphere.

Q-175. What is oxygen cycle?
Ans. It is the continuous production and consumption of atmospheric oxygen by a living organism of the earth in such a way that a balance is maintained.

Q-176. What is pollution?
Ans. Pollution is the contamination of the environment which results in potential hazards to the well-being of living organisms of the earth.

Q-177. What are different types of pollution?
Ans. Pollution can be broadly classified into these categories: air pollution, water pollution, land pollution, noise pollution and radioactive pollution.

Q-178. What are the two main causes of pollution in today's world?
Ans. Population explosion and excessive industrialisation are the two main causes of pollution in today's world.

Q-179. Name any two major pollutant chemicals.
Ans. Carbon monoxide (CO) and sulphur dioxide (SO_2).

Q-180. What is biomass?
Ans. It is an organic matter used as a source of energy.

Q-181. What do you understand by birth rate?
Ans. Birth rate is the number of births that take place every year.

Q-182. What is the unit used to measure the intensity of sound?
Ans. Decibel is used as a unit to measure the intensity of sound.

Q-183. What do you understand by denudation?
Ans. It is the wear and tear of rocks due to natural atmospheric causes.

Q-184. What is chlorination?
Ans. The application of chlorine to water to purify it to make it fit for human consumption is called chlorination.

Q-185. What is desalination?
Ans. It is the removal of salt from water.

Q-186. Which country is called the land of windmills?
Ans. The Netherlands.

Q-187. What is Silicon?
Ans. Silicon is an element naturally found in rocks in the form of silicates.

Q-188. What is Silicon mainly used for?
Ans. Silicon is mainly used for making microprocessor chips used in computers.

Q-189. How many mammal species are there in the world?
Ans. There are approximately 400 species of mammals in the world.

Q-190. What are biorhythms?
Ans. Biological cycles that occur in living beings are called biorhythms. For example, heartbeats.

Q-191. How old is the Earth?
Ans. The earth is about 4600 million years old.

Q-192. What does the term 'range of tolerance' mean?
Ans. The term 'range of tolerance' of a living organism means the range of environmental conditions within which it can survive and flourish.

Q-193. What is the bionomial system of nomenclature?
Ans. It is system of naming all organisms in terms of their genus and species.

Q-194. Who developed the bionomial system of nomenclature?
Ans. Linnaeus, a biologist, developed the bionomial system of nomenclature.

Q-195. What is ecological succession?
Ans. The gradual but continuous change in a community is called ecological succession.

Q-196. What do you understand by the ice age?
Ans. The ice age was a period in the earth's history when large areas were covered by sheets of ice.

Q-197. How many ice ages have been there on earth?
Ans. There have been three ice ages on the earth.

Q-198. Which animal was first domesticated by humans?
Ans. Dog.

Q-199. How many different species of fish are there?
Ans. There are over 21,000 different species of fish.

Q-200. Why do certain animals go extinct?
Ans. Animals go extinct when they are not able to adapt to the changing environment.

Q-201. How was coal formed?
Ans. Coal was formed when plant debris began to accumulate and decompose under high pressure over millions of years.

Q-202. What are meteorological factors of environment?
Ans. Sunlight, rainfall, humidity, temperature and wind are meteorological factors that affect the environment.

Q-203. What is carbon monoxide?
Ans. Carbon monoxide is a colourless, odourless gas that is produced by the incomplete combustion of carbon-based fuels.

Q-204. How can carbon monoxide affect human beings?
Ans. Carbon monoxide lowers the amount of oxygen that enters our blood. It also slows down reflexes.

Q-205. How is lead a pollutant?
Ans. Lead is present in petrol, diesel, paints, etc. When inhaled, it can cause damage to the nervous system. It also results in digestive problems.

Q-206. How is ozone a pollutant?
Ans. Although the layer of ozone present in the stratosphere shields the earth from ultraviolet radiations, on ground-level, ozone has toxic effects on human beings, causing low resistance, pneumonia.

Q-207. Why is nitrogen oxide (NO_2) emitted from burning fuels harmful to the environment?
Ans. Nitrogen oxide emitted from burning fuels causes *smog* and *acid rain*.

Q-208. What does SPM stand for?
Ans. SPM stands for Suspended Particulate Matter.

Q-209. What is SPM?
Ans. SPM is the solid remains of smoke, dust and vapour that stay in the air for long periods.

Q-210. What ill-effects does SPM cause?
Ans. SPM reduces visibility and causes respiratory problems.

Q-211. Which law has been enacted by the Indian Government to control and prevent air pollution?
Ans. The Air (Prevention and Control of Pollution) Act was enacted in 1981 to provide for the prevention, control and abatement of air pollution in India.

Q-212. Which law has been enacted by the Indian Government for the control and prevention of water pollution?
Ans. The Water (Prevention and Control of Pollution) Act was enacted in 1974 to provide for the prevention and control of water pollution, and for maintaining or restoring of wholesomeness of water in the country.

Q-213. What is the Environment (Protection) Act?
Ans. The Environment (Protection) Act is an act enacted by the Indian Government in 1986 with the objective of providing for the protection and improvement of the environment.

Q-214. Has the Indian Government enacted any law regarding cruelty towards animals?
Ans. Yes. The Indian Government enacted the Prevention of Cruelty to Animals Act in 1960 to prevent the infliction of unnecessary pain or suffering on animals.

Q-215. Which Indian law protects the wildlife against poaching and other illegal activities?

Ans. The Wildlife (Protection) Act passed in 1972 by the Indian Government protects wildlife against poaching and other illegal activities.

Q-216. Which law protects the rights of scheduled tribes living in Indian forests?

Ans. The Scheduled Tribes and Other Traditional Forest Dwellers (Recognition of Forest Rights) Act, 2006 protects the rights of scheduled tribes living in Indian forests.

Q-217. What is the aim of the Forest Conservation Act enacted by the Indian Government in 1980?

Ans. The aim of the Forest Conservation Act enacted in 1980 by the Indian Government is to help conserve the country's forests.

Q-218. What do you understand by biological diversity?

Ans. Biological diversity is the variety of living organisms found within a specified geographic region or ecosystem.

Q-219. Why is it important to maintain biological diversity within ecosystems?

Ans. Different elements of an ecosystem are not only interdependent for their survival, together they also form a web of complex interactions that helps an ecosystem achieve stability.

Q-220. What is the Convention on Biological Diversity?

Ans. The Convention on Biological Diversity (CBD) is a global agreement initiated by the United Nations Environment Programme (UNEP) and entered into force on 29 December, 1993 to conserve biological diversity in the world.

Q-221. Which day is celebrated as the International Day for Biological Diversity?

Ans. 22 May.

Q-222. What percentage of earth's water is fresh?
Ans. Only 3 % of the earth's water is fresh.

Q-223. How can ground water get contaminated?
Ans. Due to landfills and septic tanks filled with waste, ground water too gets contaminated.

Q-224. What is a tributary?
Ans. A tributary is a small river or stream flowing into a bigger river.

Q-225. What is evaporation?
Ans. Evaporation is the natural process in which water gets heated by the sun and turns into water vapour.

Q-226. What is condensation?
Ans. Condensation is the process in which water vapour cools down and turns back into liquid.

Q-227. What is soil erosion?
Ans. Soil erosion is the wearing down or washing down of the soil due to water, wind, etc.

Q-228. What do you understand by hydrologic cycle?
Ans. A hydrologic cycle is a natural cycle in which water circulates from the atmosphere to the land and the ocean and then back again.

Q-229. What do you understand by infiltration?
Ans. When water moves down through the earth's surface, it is called infiltration.

Q-230. Define watershed.
Ans. A watershed is the area drained by a river and its tributaries.

Q-231. What is a wetland?
Ans. A wetland is a water saturated land where aquatic plants and animals live.

Q-232. What does Environmental Science consist of?
Ans. Environmental Science consists of physical, chemical, biological interaction between the different components of the environment.

Q-233. What do you understand by the Earth Summit?
Ans. The Earth Summit was a major United Nations conference held in Rio de Janeiro from 3 June to 14 June, 1992 in order to highlight the earth's biological diversity and the importance of preserving the environment.

Q-234. Which is the largest tributary of the Ganga River?
Ans. Ghaghara River.

Q-235. Which mountain does the Ganga River originate from?
Ans. The Ganga River originates from a cave at Gaumukh in the Himalayas.

Q-236. What are hydrophytes?
Ans. Hydrophytes are plants that grow in water.

Q-237. What are mesophytes?
Ans. Mesophytes are plants with average water requirements.

Q-238. What are xerophytes?
Ans. Xerophytes are plants that grow in dry environments amid shortage of water.

Q-239. Give one example of hydrophytes.
Ans. Water Lilies.

Q-240. Give one example of a mesophyte.
Ans. A rose plant.

Q-241. Name one xerophyte.
Ans. Cactii.

Q-242. Define spatial studies.
Ans. Spatial study is the study of organisms with their immediate surroundings.

Q-243. Which environmental studies related directive was issued by the Supreme Court of India in 1991?
Ans. In 1991, the Supreme Court of India issued a directive making all curricula environment-oriented.

Q-244. What is the full form of CEE?
Ans. It stands for Centre for Environment Education.

Q-245. What are the objectives of CEE?
Ans. Its primary objective is to improve public awareness and understanding of the environmental issues.

Q-246. Which ministry was CEE set up by?
Ans. CEE was set up by the Ministry of Environment.

Q-247. What do you understand by habitat diversity?
Ans. The range of habitats present in a given region is a measure of its habitat diversity.

Q-248. What is habitat disruption?
Ans. Habitat disruption is a disturbance of the physical environment in which a population lives.

NATURAL RESOURCES

Q-249. How are natural resources generally classified?
Ans. They can be classified as following: forest resource, water resource, mineral resource, food resource, energy resource and land resource.

Q-250. What is FSI?
Ans. FSI stands for Forest Survey of India.

Q-251. What is the main objective of FSI?
Ans. Its main objective is to assess the forest cover of the country biannually.

Q-252. What is TOF?
Ans. TOF stands for Trees Outside Forests.

Q-253. What do you understand by TOF?
Ans. TOF (Trees Outside Forests) is a factor taken into consideration by the Forest Survey of India (FSI) during its assessment of the country's forest cover.

Q-254. What are thematic maps?
Ans. Thematic maps of a region depict forest types, major species composition and crown density of the forests.

Q-255. What do you mean by shift agriculture?
Ans. Shift agriculture is a traditional method of agriculture in which a small area is occupied by clearing forests to raise crops for a few years and abandon the land later.

Q-256. Is shift agriculture harmful to the environment?
Ans. Yes, because after the abandonment, the forest does not grow back at the same rate.

Q-257. What is a forest fire?
Ans. A forest fire is usually a natural phenomenon in which a fire breaks out in the forest and spreads all over with the help of wind.

Q-258. Which planet is called the blue planet?
Ans. The Earth is called the blue planet.

Q-259. Why is the earth called the blue planet?
Ans. The earth is called the blue planet because two-third of the planet is covered with water.

Q-260. What is the full form of WHO?
Ans. WHO stands for World Health Organization.

Q-261. Which place receives the maximum rainfall every year?
Ans. Mount Waialeale in Hawaii.

Q-262. Which place in India receives maximum rainfall?
Ans. Mawsynram in Meghalaya.

The Earth

Q-263. What is surface runoff?

Ans. Surface runoff refers to the overflow of water that occurs when the soil of that region is infiltrated to maximum capacity.

Q-264. Why do floods happen?

Ans. Floods are caused when there are intense storms which produce more runoff than an area can store or a stream can carry within its normal channel.

Q-265. What are landslides?

Ans. Landslides are mass movement of soil downhill.

Q-266. What do you understand by mulching?
Ans. Mulching is the practice of covering of soil with plants.

Q-267. What is organic farming?
Ans. The practice of farming with increased organic input to the soil is called organic farming.

Q-268. Who started the Chipko Movement?
Ans. The Chipko Movement was started by Sunder Lal Bahuguna.

Q-269. What do you understand by Chipko Movement?
Ans. The Chipko Movement was a resistance movement against deforestation that began in the Uttarakhand region in India in 1970s. In this movement, the locals hugged the trees to prevent them from being cut.

Q-270. What is drainage?
Ans. Drainage is the draining of accumulated water through runoff to avoid soil saturation.

Q-271. What is eutrophication?
Ans. Eutrophication is the presence of excessive nutrients in a marine environment.

Q-272. Why is eutrophication an environmental problem?
Ans. Increased nutrients result in excessive growth of algae on the surface of the water body, which in turn results in cutting off significant amount of oxygen from reaching the aquatic animals.

Q-273. Who floated the term 'ecological succession'?
Ans. Ragnar Hult floated the term 'ecological succession' in 1985.

Q-274. What is ecological pyramid?
Ans. It is a graphical representation of the ecological parameters with producers (plants) forming the base and carnivores at the top.

Q-275. What are lava tubes?
Ans. These are caves underneath which lava flows.

Questions & Answers

Q-276. Where were lava tubes discovered?
Ans. Lava tubes were discovered in Hawaii in 1960s.

Q-277. What do you understand by ornamental plants?
Ans. Ornamental plants are plants used for indoor/outdoor decor and horticultural purposes.

Q-278. What is the total area of India?
Ans. The total area of India is about 32,87,263 sq km.

Q-279. What is the latitudinal and longitudinal dimension of India?
Ans. India stretches from 8 degrees 4 minutes to 37 degrees 6 minutes N latitude and from 68 degrees 7 minutes to 97 degrees 25 minutes E longitude.

Q-280. What is in situ conservation?
Ans. In situ or on-site conservation refers to the maintenance and use of wild plant population in the habitats, where they naturally occur, without any interference from human beings.

Q-281. What is ex-situ conservation?
Ans. Ex-situ, also off-site conservation, is a type of conservation in which the preservation and culture takes place outside the production system.

Q-282. What is alpha diversity?
Ans. Alpha diversity is the number of species in a specified area.

Q-283. What is beta diversity?
Ans. Beta diversity is the diversity between area along a given habitat or gradient.

Q-284. What is endemic species?
Ans. Endemic species are those species which are limited to a particular area.

Q-285. What do you understand by exotic species?
Ans. A species introduced from another country is termed as an exotic species.

Q-286. What is gamma diversity?
Ans. Gamma diversity is the diversity of habitats within a particular geographical area.

Q-287. What is genetic diversity?
Ans. Genetic diversity is the variation that occurs within a species due to a new combination of genes.

Q-288. What is quinine?
Ans. Quinine is a white alkaloid used for medicinal purposes.

Q-289. Where is quinine obtained from?
Ans. Quinine is obtained from Cinchona trees.

Q-290. What does IUCN stand for?
Ans. IUCN stands for International Union for Conservation of Nature.

Q-291. When was IUCN formed?
Ans. IUCN was formed in 1948 as the world's first environmental organisation.

Q-292. What is red data book?
Ans. A red data book is a list of endangered species of plants and animals.

Q-293. Which organisation releases red data book every year?
Ans. International Union for Conservation of Nature (IUCN).

Q-294. What is smog?
Ans. Smog is the mixture of smoke and fog.

Q-295. What is the chemical formula of ozone gas?
Ans. O_3.

Q-296. What is necrosis?
Ans. Necrosis is the dead area of a leaf caused by air pollution.

Q-297. What is chlorosis?
Ans. Chlorosis is the unnatural yellowing of leaves caused by air pollution.

Q-298. What is epinasty?
Ans. Epinasty is the unnatural curling of the leaves caused by air pollution.

Q-299. What is abscission?
Ans. Abscission is the premature dropping of leaves caused by air pollution.

Q-300. What is the effect of higher concentration of sulphur dioxide (SO_2) in plants?
Ans. Stiffness in flower buds and their premature falling are some of the results of higher concentration of sulphur dioxide in plants.

Q-301. What is the effect of sulphur dioxide on humans?
Ans. Sulphur dioxide causes chest constriction, headache, vomiting and may even cause death.

Q-302. What is the effect of hydrogen sulphide (H_2S) on human body?
Ans. Hydrogen sulphide causes irritation in eyes and throat. It also causes nausea.

Q-303. What is the effect of carbon monoxide (CO) on humans?
Ans. Carbon monoxide reduces the oxygen carrying capacity of blood, and results in poisoning.

Q-304. What is the effect of hydrogen cyanide (HCN) on humans?
Ans. Hydrogen cyanide affects the nerve cells, and causes dry throat, blurred vision and headaches.

Q-305. What is the effect of ammonia (NH_3) on humans?
Ans. Ammonia causes inflammation in the respiratory tract.

Q-306. What is SLO?
Ans. SLO stands for Suspended Living Organisms.

Q-307. What is the effect of SLO on humans?
Ans. SLO causes various allergies in the respiratory tract, eyes, nose and skin.

Q-308. Give examples of SPM.
Ans. Soot, Ash and Smoke are common examples of SPM.

Q-309. What is the effect of volatile organics?
Ans. Volatile organics can cause irritation of the eyes, nose and throat.

Q-310. What is adsorption?
Ans. Adsorption is the physical process in which liquid and gas particles get attached to a solid surface.

Q-311. Give one example of adsorption.
Ans. Chalk powder on a duster.

Q-312. What is incineration?
Ans. Incineration is the process in which a combustible material present in a waste gas is burnt or oxidised using a special apparatus.

Q-313. What is absorption?
Ans. When liquid or gas particles get soaked by a solid substance, it is called absorption.

Q-314. Give one example of absorption.
Ans. Resin soaked in water.

Q-315. What does RO stand for?
Ans. RO stands for Reverse Osmosis.

Q-316. What is soil pollution?
Ans. Soil pollution is the degradation of soil by various human or non-human factors.

Q-317. Name some factors which are responsible for soil pollution.
Ans. Some factors responsible for soil polution are industrial pollutants, urban waste, radioactive waste and unsuitable agricultural practices.

Q-318. What do you understand by noise pollution?
Ans. Noise pollution can be defined as unwanted, undesirable sounds added to the atmosphere without any regard to their harmful effects.

Q-319. What is the most common unit for measuring sound?
Ans. Decibel is the most common unit for measuring sound.

Q-320. What is the range of sound in decibels to which human ear shows sensitivity?
Ans. Human ear is sensitive to a sound range of 0 to 180 decibels.

Q-321. Who contributes the most towards noise pollution?
Ans. Noise pollution generated by human beings is the foremost factor contributing to noise pollution.

Q-322. What are the basic effects of noise pollution on human beings?
Ans. The basic effects of noise pollution are audiological, biological and behavioural.

Q-323. What is the audiological effect of noise pollution?
Ans. The audiological effect is the unsatisfactory performance of hearing mechanism in humans due to noise pollution.

Q-324. What is the biological effect of noise pollution?
Ans. The biological effect is when noise pollution starts interfering with the functioning of the bodies of living beings.

Q-325. What is the behavioural effect of noise pollution?
Ans. The behavioural effect is when noise pollution interferes with the social functioning of a person.

Q-326. Name some common diseases caused by noise pollution.
Ans. Heart problems, high blood pressure, impaired hearing, etc.

Q-327. Mention two elements used in radioactive generators.
Ans. Uranium and Plutonium.

Q-328. What is cosmic radiation?
Ans. Cosmic radiation is the radiation coming from outside the solar system.

Q-329. What is sonic barrier?
Ans. The velocity of sound is also termed as sonic barrier.

Q-330. What do you understand by sonic boom?
Ans. Sonic boom is a phenomenon where a solid body breaks the sound barrier and therefore creates powerful waves of sound which are capable of shattering glasses.

Q-331. What is algae bloom?
Ans. Algae bloom is the rapid increase of aquatic algae due to eutrophication.

Q-332. Which element causes minamata disease?
Ans. Mercury (Hg) causes minamata disease.

Q-333. What is acid rain?
Ans. Acid rain is a rain or any other form of precipitation that is unusually acidic, meaning that it possesses a high level of ionised hydrogen.

Q-334. What is sustainable development?
Ans. The systematic and successful management of resources to meet the needs of the present without compromising the requirements of future generations is called sustainable development.

Q-335. What is consumerism?
Ans. Consumerism is the belief that it is good to buy and consume a lot of goods and services.

Q-336. When and where was the concept of sustainable development adopted globally?
Ans. The concept of sustainable development was adopted at the Earth Summit in Rio de Janeiro, Brazil.

Q-337. How do CFCs affect environment?
Ans. CFCs or Chlorofluorocarbons rise to the stratosphere and are mainly responsible for the depletion of ozone layer.

Q-338. What is geothermal energy?
Ans. Energy generated by the hot rocks beneath the surface of the earth is called geothermal energy.

Q-339. What effect does global warming have on glaciers?
Ans. Global warming melts glaciers and increases the sea level.

Q-340. What do you understand by monoculture?
Ans. The cultivation of genetically identical crops over a given area is called monoculture.

Q-341. What is natality rate?
Ans. Natality rate is defined as the number of births per 1000 individuals of a population per year.

Q-342. What is mortality rate?
Ans. Mortality rate is defined as the number of deaths per 1000 individuals of a population per year.

Q-343. What do you understand by immigration?
Ans. It is the movement of a group or individuals from other regions into a particular country.

Q-344. What do you understand by emigration?
Ans. It is the movement of a group or individuals from a country to regions outside.

Q-345. Which organism causes tuberculosis?
Ans. Mycobacterium tuberculosis causes tuberculosis.

Q-346. When was the Universal Declaration of Human Rights adopted by the United Nations?
Ans. The Universal Declaration of Human Rights was adopted by the United Nations on December 10, 1948.

Q-347. What is the full form of UNESCO?
Ans. UNESCO stands for United Nations Educational, Scientific and Cultural Organization.

Q-348. How does marine pollution occur?
Ans. Marine pollution occurs when harmful chemical particles, industrial, agricultural and residential wastes enter the oceans.

Q-349. What is marine pollution?
Ans. Marine pollution is when harmful chemicals enter the food web of the sea and cause mutation in marine organisms. It also can cause widespread loss of marine life. For example, oil spills.

Q-350. What is the full form of DDT?
Ans. DDT stands for dichorodiphenyltrichloroethane.

Q-351. When was DDT first banned and where?
Ans. DDT was first banned in the United States in 1972.

Q-352. What is the effect of DDT on human beings?
Ans. DDT can cause genotoxicity in human beings.

Q-353. What is genotoxicity?
Ans. Genotoxicity is a deleterious action on a cell's genetic material affecting its integrity.

FILL IN THE BLANKS

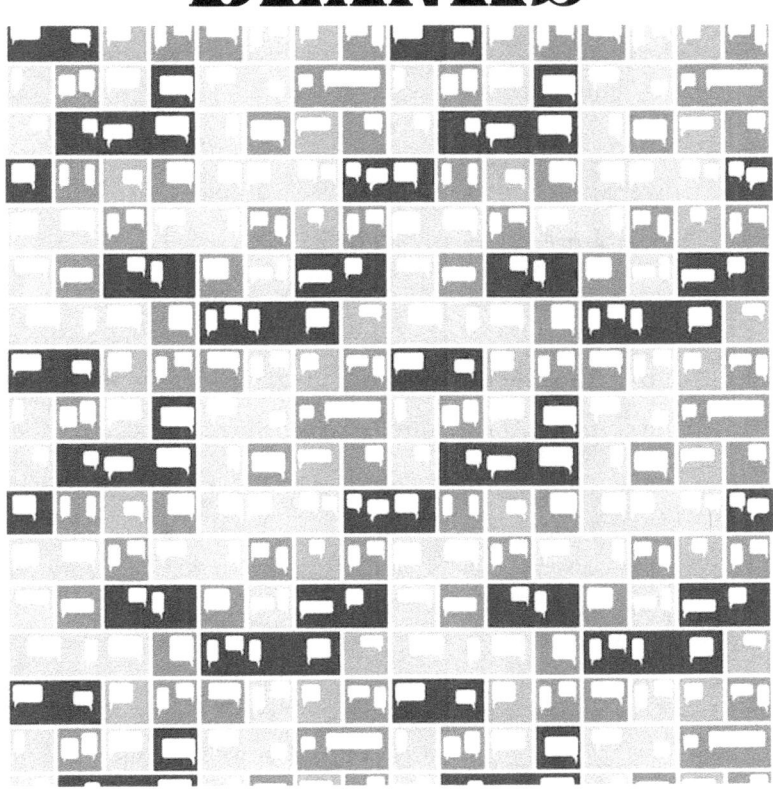

Fill in the Blanks

1. Lack of vegetation leads to _____ erosion.

2. The top layer of the earth is called _____.

3. The full form of WHC is _____.

4. The removal of trees is known as _____.

5. _____ often leads to soil erosion.

6. The two types of _____ resources are renewable and non-renewable resources.

7. Fossil fuel is a _____ natural resource.

8. Water and wind are _____ natural resources.

9. One example of a toxic metal is _____.

10. The contamination of air / water / land is known as _____.

11. Carbon dioxide and methane are two _____ gases.

12. The combination of smoke and fog is called _____.

13. The pore on the surface of a leaf through which gases pass is called _____.

14. Plants convert _____ to oxygen.

15. The Ozone layer shields the earth from _____ rays.

16. _____ is a colourless gas.

17. _____ is an odourless gas.

18. _____ is the father of Green Revolution.

Fill in the Blanks

19. Increased _____ production during the late 1960s led to the Green revolution.

20. _____ per cent of water on the earth is salty.

21. HYV seeds stands for _____ seeds.

22. World Cancer Day is celebrated on _____.

23. _____ is a natural air pollutant.

24. _____ is a device used to control air pollutants.

25. ESP stands for _____.

26. Change in the temperature of water bodies due to human activities results in _____ pollution.

27. Two major causes of water pollution are _____ and _____.

28. The science of cultivating plants is called_____.

29. Increased nutrients in water bodies is called _____.

30. Two examples of _____ disasters are floods and earthquakes.

31. The increasing atmospheric temperature is called _____.

32. Altering the earth's environmental conditions mechanically is called _____.

33. Rain that contains carbon dioxide, sulphur dioxide and nitrogen oxide is known as _____ rain.

34. The _____ in London happened in the year, 1952.

35. The Bhopal Gas Tragedy in India occurred in the year, _____.

36. The leakage of methyl _____ led to the Bhopal Gas tragedy.

37. Mercury poisoning leads to the _____ disease.

38. Underwater calcium carbonate structures are known as _____.

39. The Great Barrier Reef is located in the _____ Sea, Australia.

40. The condition of having excess fat in the body is called _____.

41. Injury or illness which happens as a result of one's working environment is called _____ hazard.

42. Hydrogen and ammonia are _____ fuels.

43. Like human beings, whales are also _____.

44. One example of an occupational disease is _____.

45. The process by which arable land turns in to a desert is called _____.

46. A _____ is an area occupied largely by trees.

47. A person's weight and height is used to calculate his _____.

48. _____ is the process of converting food in to energy for the body.

49. _____ and Catabolism are the two kinds of Metabolism.

50. _____ is the process in plants that uses carbon dioxide and water to make glucose and oxygen.

51. The green pigment in plants is called _____.

52. _____ is the cultivation of forests.

Fill in the Blanks

53. _____ is a combination of methane and carbon dioxide produced by anaerobes.

54. _____ is the organelle where photosynthesis in a plant takes place.

55. The process of breaking molecules to produce energy in the body is known as _____.

56. The opposite of _____ is Anabolism.

57. _____ is also known as 'Blue Green Algae'.

58. Undesirable sounds that affect the health of living beings is called _____ Pollution.

59. The process of _____ uses microorganisms to remove contaminants.

60. Sheet erosion is a type of _____ erosion.

61. A _____ is a small valley formed as a result of erosion of land by water .

62. A _____ is used to remove oil from water.

63. Substances used to control or kill pests are called _____.

64. Fungi that cause skin diseases are called _____.

65. The Wildlife Trust of India is located in _____.

66. _____ National Park is the oldest national park in India.

67. The _____ cavefish is an example of a critically endangered fish.

68. The costliest natural disaster happened recently in _____.

69. Growth of vegetation in water bodies due to excess of nutrients is known as _____.

70. CFC stands for _____.

71. _____ is the largest importer of illegal wildlife trading.

72. Water bodies in which oxygen is reducing is called _____ waters.

73. Decline in the population of bees has led to _____ decline.

74. The population of _____ has reduced significantly due to pesticides.

75. The illegal catching/killing of animals is known as _____.

76. Blue whale and snow leopard are examples of _____ species.

A blue whale.

77. Any living organism that does not exist is known to be _____.

78. The Earth Hour is observed in the month of _____.

Fill in the Blanks

79. Approximately _____ countries participated in the earth hour in year 2011.

80. The 'Great Pacific Garbage Patch' is a patch of high concentration of _____ in the North Pacific Ocean.

81. Polyvinyl alcohol is a _____ plastic.

82. Abundance of _____ in a water body is called algal bloom.

83. Accumulation of a substance as it moves further up the food chain is known as _____.

84. Chernobyl disaster of 1986 happened in _____.

85. The biggest man-made forest in the world is in _____.

86. The discovery of DDT as an insecticide was made by _____.

87. DDT stands for _____.

88. Diabetes, asthma, obesity and depression are known to be _____ diseases.

89. The population density is higher in _____ areas.

90. The Green Wall of China is a _____ forest in China.

91. The Gobi desert is located in _____.

92. The largest desert in the world is the _____ desert.

93. Lead and mercury are examples of _____ metals.

94. _____ are used to get rid of weeds.

95. Blood, catheters, gloves, syringes, dead bodies are _____ waste.

96. Ozone layer is found in the _____.

97. Ozone is made up of three _____ atoms.

98. The two main constituents of air are oxygen and _____.

99. The spread of a disease across a large area (eg. countries or continents) is called a _____.

100. The disease restricted to a small region is called an _____.

101. Hailstones, rain, and snow are different forms of _____.

102. _____ is known to receive the lowest rainfall in India.

103. The _____ can be found at the Kaziranga National Park.

104. The _____ National Park is located in Assam, India.

105. A _____ is a very strong snowstorm.

Kaziranga National Park

Fill in the Blanks

106. An abrupt fall in temperature is called a _____ wave.

107. An _____ is a temporary shelter built from snow.

108. Frostbite of the skin happens as a result of excess _____.

109. The process of extracting metal from its ore is called _____.

110. Paper is made from the _____ plant.

111. _____ are substances that are known to cause cancer.

112. Asbestos is an example of a _____.

113. The largest producer of tobacco is _____.

114. The World Health Organisation (WHO) was formed in the year, _____.

115. Air that rotates at a very high speed causing destruction is known as a _____.

116. The WWF stands for _____.

117. Charcoal made from biomass is called _____.

118. The full form of LPG is _____.

119. LPG is composed of _____ and butane.

120. Natural gas consists of mainly ethane and _____.

121. _____ is a popular alternative to petrol and diesel.

122. The population of the world is approximately_____ billion.

123. The _____ revolution between 18th and 19th centuries happened in England.

124. _____ bombs were dropped in the cities of Hiroshima and Nagasaki, Japan in 1945.

125. The 2011 earthquake in Japan was _____ on the Richter scale.

126. Air pollution is mainly caused by _____.

127. The full form of SPM is _____.

128. The largest continent in the world is _____.

129. The hunting of whales is known as _____.

130. The third most populated country in the world is _____.

131. International Whaling Commission was established in the year _____.

132. The process of digging out ores form the earth is called _____.

133. The Hirakud dam is built over the river _____ in Orissa.

134. _____ are used to store water and prevent its overflow on land.

Hirakund Dam

Fill in the Blanks

135. Water in the gaseous state is called _____.

136. The Gir forest in Gujarat is a home to the _____.

137. The Blue-billed duck is found in _____.

138. Ocean water is more _____ than freshwater.

139. Trout, salmon and eels are examples of _____ fishes.

140. _____ are used to supply plants with nutrients.

141. _____ is an example of a natural fertilizer.

142. _____ farming restricts usage of chemical fertilizers and pesticides.

143. _____ plants are used as organic fertilizers due to their ability to fix nitrogen from the atmosphere.

144. The outermost layer of the earth containing the crust and upper mantle is known as _____.

145. Two examples of _____ disasters that happen on the surface of the earth are earthquakes and volcanoes.

146. The liquid that bursts out of a volcano is called_____.

147. The most recent, powerful volcanic eruption in 1815 took place in Mount _____, Indonesia .

148. _____ is the second highest mountain in the world after Mount Everest.

149. Reuse of electronic items is called _____.

150. Global _____ is being dumped in countries like India and Africa.

151. Discarded computers and television sets are examples of _____ waste.

152. The Prairie is a flat area of grassland without tress, and is commonly found in _____.

153. Land used for grazing is called _____ land.

154. Animals tamed for domestic purposes are called _____.

155. Plants eaten by livestock animals are called _____.

156. _____ is when animals eat forage.

157. _____ sometimes leads to desertification or soil erosion.

158. Cows, pigs and horses are examples of _____.

159. Millions of sharks are killed every year for their _____.

160. _____ is a delicacy in Asia.

161. PETA stands for _____.

162. Excessive irrigation may lead to increase in the _____ of soil.

163. The National Zoological Park is located in _____.

164. _____ refers to the depletion of nutrients in soil that dissolve in water due to excessive irrigation.

165. Water below the surface of the earth is called _____.

166. Timber is also known as _____.

167. Wood used for construction is called _____.

168. About _____ per cent of the land on earth is covered by forests.

169. The point where freshwater and the sea meet is called a/an _____.

170. The two kinds of aquatic systems are – marine ecosystem and _____ ecosystem.

Fill in the Blanks

171. Two examples of _____ are swamps and marshes.

172. Duckweed is an example of a _____ plant.

173. _____ energy is dependent on sunlight.

174. The water that flows into land leads to a _____.

175. Floods can cause _____ diseases.

176. Cholera and dysentery are diseases that come from drinking _____ water.

177. Power produced from energy of falling water is called _____.

178. _____ is produced from hydropower.

179. Tidal energy, wind energy and solar energy are examples of _____ energy.

180. The _____ Movement started in 1970s, in India.

181. The Sardar Sarovar Dam is on the _____ River, Gujarat.

182. Medha Patkar and Baba Amte are associated with the _____.

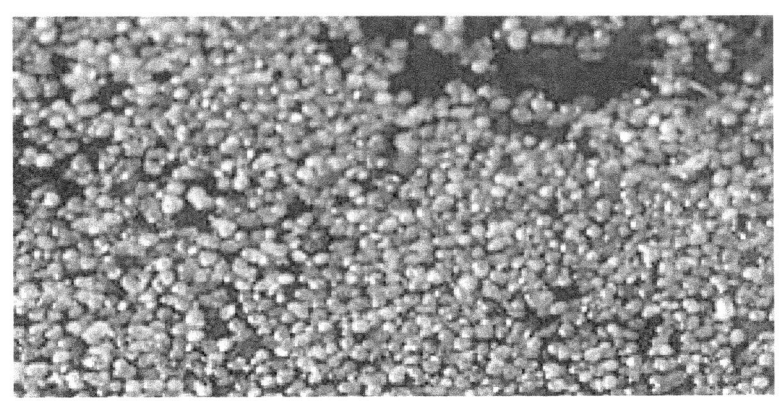

Duckweed plant

183. The _____ Movement popularised hugging of trees to prevent them from being cut.

184. _____ was the leader of the Chipko Movement .

185. 'Ecology is Permanent Economy' is a slogan related to the _____ Movement.

186. The _____ of population is a major problem while building dams.

187. Urbanisation has led to human _____.

188. The _____ Butterfly is famous for its migration from Canada to Mexico.

189. _____ occurs when birds migrate in the wrong direction due to faulty programming.

190. A _____ is employed to look after cattle.

191. HMS stands for _____.

192. Pomfret, swordfish, sharks and dolphins are some examples of _____.

193. Movement in the same direction by animals, birds, fish, etc. is called _____.

194. Birds swarming is called _____.

Pomfret

Fill in the Blanks

195. _____ is when cattle swarm.

196. _____ migration is primarily due to weather conditions and food availability.

197. Transferring livestock seasonally for the purpose of grazing is known as _____.

198. Western sandpiper and pink-footed goose are examples of _____ birds.

199. Butterflies and moths are examples of insects that migrate _____.

200. The care of livestock for the purpose of agriculture is known as _____.

201. _____ flu in 1918 killed approximately 50 million people.

202. On 12 January 2010, the powerful earthquake in _____ took place.

203. _____ are swarming grasshoppers that destroy crops.

204. _____ are short plants with multiple wood stems and look like bushes.

205. Gangotri, Siachen and Rathong are names of Indian _____.

206. The Vienna Conference held in Austria took place in the year _____.

207. The HCFC stands for _____.

208. The HCFC is a refrigerant that contributes to _____ depletion.

209. _____ is the second most populated continent.

210. Better _____ opportunities is one of the major reasons for immigration.

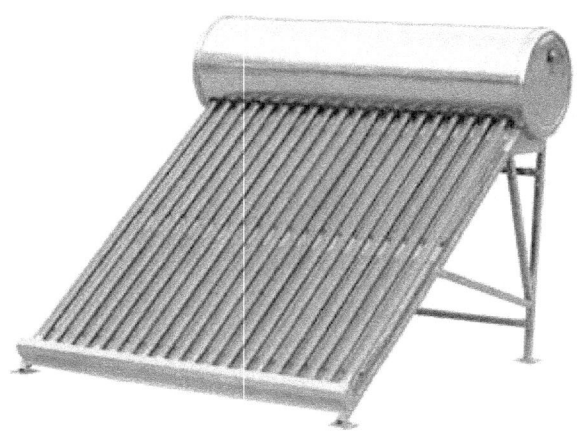

A solar water heater

211. Improved _____ facilities is one of the reasons for population growth.

212. Solar cooker and solar water heater use the energy derived from _____.

213. _____ tillage is practised to prevent soil erosion.

214. _____ planning is one way to limit the ever increasing human population.

215. The partition of India in 1947 led to mass _____ on the basis of religion.

216. Labour migration during industrialisation happened in the form of _____.

217. _____ can be found in the troposphere and stratosphere.

218. Ozone is known to cause mostly _____ diseases.

219. Overconsumption results in _____ depletion.

Fill in the Blanks

220. Growing one type of crop on a field is called _____.

221. Crop rotation is a method used in _____ agriculture.

222. _____ is the method of rotating crops on a field every year to maintain the quality of soil.

223. Both water and wind can lead to _____ erosion.

224. _____ energy uses the energy of tides.

225. Two examples of natural pollution are _____ and wildfires.

226. Two examples of wildfires are _____ and bushfires.

227. Bushfires are most commonly found in _____.

228. _____ fever takes place as a result of exposure to pollen.

229. The _____ of 1910 is also known as 'The Big Burn/Blow up'.

230. 'The big blow up' burnt about _____ acres in Montana, Washington and Idaho, lasted for 36 hours and killed 87 people and 78 firefighters.

231. The largest land carnivore is _____.

232. The fastest animal on land is the _____.

233. The _____ is the largest coral reef in the world.

234. The largest animal in the world is the _____.

235. The largest land animal is the _____.

236. The extinct species of _____ is related to elephants.

237. The two types of elephants are the African Elephant and the _____ Elephant.

238. The _____ of whales is used to produce whale oil.

239. Whales are hunted mostly for their _____.

240. The trading of tusks is called _____ trade, it is an illegal trade.

241. CITES stands for _____.

242. IUCN stands for _____.

243. _____ is the largest bird.

244. _____ started the Green Belt Movement in Kenya and is the first African woman to receive the Nobel Peace Prize.

245. _____ is a documentary released in the year 2006 about Global Warming.

246. MAB stands for _____, it is a program started by UNESCO to better the relationship between people and their environment.

247. WDPA stands for _____.

248. _____ of an individual is the total amount of greenhouse gas emissions made by a person.

249. _____ is the opposite of deforestation, it is the natural or deliberate building of forests, or planting trees.

250. The paper industry also engages in _____ to replace trees that have been cut.

251. Continental _____ is the movement of continents over the surface of the earth.

252. When the layers of water in a lake do not mix, it is called a _____ lake.

253. The Lake _____ in Antarctica is an example of a Meromictic lake.

Fill in the Blanks

254. _____ is a layer in a water body that separates the surface layer from the cold bottom layer.

255. A structure built on land to reduce the effect of noise pollution is called a _____ barrier.

256. The _____ measures the salinity of water.

257. The dissolved salt in water determines its _____.

258. _____ are those plants that grow in soil water with high salt concentration.

259. Mangrove is an example of a _____.

260. ENSO stands for _____.

261. A vast area of land with natural vegetation is known as _____.

262. Except _____ every continent has wetlands.

263. A Savannah is an example of a _____.

264. Tending aquatic creatures is known as _____.

265. _____ is an example of Aquaculture.

266. The _____ is an example of GMO.

267. The full form of GMO is _____.

Mangroves

268. _____ results in the depletion of fishes in a water body.

269. The World Oceans Day is celebrated every year on the _____.

270. Fishing with a trawl is called _____.

271. The method of trawling is used to obtain fishes such as _____.

272. Fishing by the method of _____ trawling damages the seabed.

273. _____ is a calcium carbonate deposition hanging from the roof of a limestone cave.

274. _____ is a calcium carbonate deposition rising from the base of the limestone cave.

275. _____ is a frost quake that happens when frozen soil cracks.

276. The method of growing glaciers is popular in _____.

277. Bulks of ice falling rapidly down a slope is known as an _____.

278. Lahar is a type of _____.

279. The _____ Avalanche took place in Austria in the year 1999, and it was responsible for the death of 31 people .

280. Environment-friendly buildings are known as _____.

281. The study of glaciers is known as _____.

282. _____ consists of those parts of the earth's surface that are frozen.

283. A biofilter uses _____ to clean water .

Fill in the Blanks

A glacier

284. The World Population Day is celebrated on _____ every year.

285. _____ are common water pollutants that damage the marine life.

286. In green technology, ESM stands for _____.

287. A _____ weapon is used to spread radioactive substances with the motive to cause death.

288. RDD stands for _____.

289. _____ weapons are those organisms that can be used to kill people.

290. _____ is an example of a biological weapon.

291. ARS stands for _____.

292. _____ is the study of birds.

293. Green waste is an example of _____ waste.

294. The study of soil are of two kinds – Pedology and _____.

295. The study of trees is called _____.

296. The study of honeybees is known as _____.

297. _____ is the study of blood.

298. The study of insects is called _____.

299. The study of freshwater bodies is known as _____.

300. _____ is the study of fungi.

Answers

1.	Soil	19.	agricultural
2.	Crust	20.	97
3.	Water Holding Capacity	21.	High Yielding Variety
		22.	February 4
4.	Deforestation	23.	Dust
5.	Deforestation	24.	Scrubber
6.	Natural	25.	Electrostatic Precipitator
7.	Non-renewable		
8.	Renewable	26.	thermal
9.	Uranium	27.	sewage and industrial waste
10.	Pollution		
11.	Greenhouse	28.	horticulture
12.	Smog	29.	eutrophication
13.	stomata	30.	natural
14.	carbon dioxide	31.	global warming
15.	ultraviolet	32.	geoengineering
16.	Carbon dioxide	33.	acid rain
17.	Oxygen	34.	Great Smog
18.	Norman Borlaug	35.	1984

36. isocyanate	59. Bioremediation
37. Minamata	60. soil
38. Coral reefs	61. gulley
39. Coral	62. skimmer
40. Obesity	63. pesticides
41. occupational	64. Dermatophytes
42. alternative	65. New Delhi
43. mammals	66. Jim Corbett
44. asbestosis / asthma	67. Alabama
45. desertification	68. Japan
46. Forest	69. Eutrophication
47. Body Mass Index (BMI)	70. Chlorofluorocarbon
48. Metabolism	71. China
49. Anabolism	72. anoxic
50. Photosynthesis	73. pollinator
51. chlorophyll	74. bees
52. Silviculture	75. poaching
53. Biogas	76. endangered
54. Chloroplast	77. extinct
55. catabolism	78. March
56. catabolism	79. 135
57. Cyanobacteria	80. plastic
58. Noise	81. biodegradable
	82. algae

Fill in the Blanks

83. Biomagnification
84. Ukraine
85. Johannesburg
86. Paul Hermann Muller
87. Dichlorodiphenyltri-chloroethane
88. lifestyle
89. urban
90. man-made
91. China
92. Antarctic
93. toxic
94. Herbicides
95. biomedical
96. stratosphere
97. oxygen
98. nitrogen
99. pandemic
100. epidemic
101. precipitation
102. Jaisalmer
103. one-horned rhino
104. Kaziranga
105. blizzard
106. cold
107. Igloo
108. cold
109. smelting
110. papyrus
111. Carcinogens
112. carcinogen
113. China
114. 1948
115. Tornado
116. World Wildlife Fund
117. biochar
118. Liquefied Petroleum Gas
119. propane
120. methane
121. CNG
122. 7
123. industrial
124. Atomic
125. 8.9
126. automobiles / vehicles
127. Suspended Particulate Matter

128. Asia
129. whaling
130. The United States
131. 1946
132. mining
133. Mahanadi
134. Dams
135. water vapour
136. Asiatic lions
137. Australia
138. salty
139. freshwater
140. Fertilizers
141. Manure
142. Organic
143. Leguminous
144. lithosphere
145. natural
146. magma
147. Tambora
148. K2
149. e-cycling
150. e-waste
151. electronic
152. North America
153. pasture
154. livestock
155. forage
156. Grazing
157. Overgrazing
158. livestock
159. fins
160. Shark fin soup
161. People for The Ethical Treatment of Animals
162. salinity
163. New Delhi
164. Leaching
165. groundwater
166. lumber
167. timber
168. 30
169. estuary
170. freshwater
171. wetlands
172. water
173. Solar
174. flood

Fill in the Blanks

175. water-borne
176. contaminated
177. hydropower
178. Hydroelectricity
179. renewable
180. Chipko
181. Narmada
182. Narmada Bachao Andolan
183. Chipko
184. Sunderlal Bahuguna
185. Chipko
186. Displacement
187. Migration
188. Monarch
189. Reverse Migration
190. cowman
191. Highly Migratory Species
192. HMS
193. swarming
194. Flocking
195. Herding
196. Bird
197. transhumance
198. migratory birds
199. seasonally
200. animal husbandry
201. Spanish
202. Haiti
203. Locusts
204. Shrubs
205. glaciers
206. 1985
207. Hydrochloro-fluorocarbon
208. ozone
209. Africa
210. employment
211. medical
212. sunlight
213. Zero
214. Family
215. Migration
216. slave trade
217. Ozone
218. respiratory
219. resource
220. monoculture
221. sustainable

Environment Quiz Book

222. Crop Rotation
223. soil erosion
224. Tidal
225. volcanoes
226. forest fires
227. Australia
228. Hay
229. Great Fire
230. 3 million
231. Polar Bear
232. cheetah
233. Great Barrier Reef
234. blue whale
235. elephant
236. mammoth
237. Asian / Indian
238. blubber
239. meat
240. ivory
241. Convention on International Trade in Endangered Species of Wild Flora and Fauna

242. International Union for Conservation of Nature and Natural Resources
243. Ostrich
244. Wangari Maathai
245. An Inconvenient Truth
246. Man and Biosphere
247. World Database on Protected Areas
248. Carbon Footprint
249. Reforestation
250. reforestation
251. drift
252. Meromictic
253. Vanda
254. Thermocline
255. sound / noise
256. Salinometer
257. salinity
258. Halophytes
259. halophyte
260. El Nino Southern Oscillation

Fill in the Blanks

261. rangelands
262. Antarctica
263. rangeland
264. aquaculture
265. Oyster farming
266. Enviropig
267. Genetically Modified Organism
268. Overfishing
269. 8th June
270. trawling
271. shrimps / tuna
272. bottom
273. Stalactite
274. Stalagmite
275. Cryoseism
276. Pakistan
277. Avalanche
278. mudslide
279. Galtur
280. Green Buildings
281. Glaciology
282. Cryosphere
283. microorganisms
284. 11 July
285. Microplastics
286. Energy Saving Module
287. radiological
288. Radiological Dispersal Device
289. Biological
290. Bacteria
291. Acute Radiation Syndrome
292. Ornithology
293. biodegradable
294. Edaphology
295. Dendrology
296. Apiology
297. Hematology
298. Entomology
299. Limnology
300. Mycology

TRUE

&

FALSE

True & False

1. There is only one ecosystem on the earth.
   ☐ True   ☐ False

2. The number of mammal species in the world is more than that of reptiles.
   ☐ True   ☐ False

3. Plastic is non-biodegradable.
   ☐ True   ☐ False

4. A biome is bigger than an ecosystem.
   ☐ True   ☐ False

5. Over the last few centuries, there has been a constant rise in the average temperature of the earth's atomosphere and oceans, called the Global Warming.
   ☐ True   ☐ False

6. The atmospheric activities that determine the weather happen mostly in the stratosphere.
   ☐ True   ☐ False

7. Ecosystem is made up both living as well as non-living elements.
   ☐ True   ☐ False

8. Ecological balance is disturbed by excessive plantation.
   ☐ True   ☐ False

9. In an ecosystem, bacteria, fungi and insects can act as decomposers.
   ☐ True   ☐ False

10. Herbivores can consume other animals too.

    ☐ True   ☐ False

11. Plants can be carnivorous too.

    ☐ True   ☐ False

12. The Sundew plant is an example of a carnivorous plant.

    ☐ True   ☐ False

13. Rats are omnivores.

    ☐ True   ☐ False

14. In a food web, same kind of plant or animal can be eaten by more than one kind of animal.

    ☐ True   ☐ False

15. Fungi and bacteria also contain chlorophyll.

    ☐ True   ☐ False

Sundew plant

True & False

16. Parasites are always harmful for the host plant or animal.

    ☐ True   ☐ False

17. Plants are the only living beings that produce their own food.

    ☐ True   ☐ False

18. Chlorophyll helps plants in photosynthesis.

    ☐ True   ☐ False

19. In a food pyramid, energy associated with the food increases with every step upwards.

    ☐ True   ☐ False

20. Water and air are biotic components of the biosphere.

    ☐ True   ☐ False

21. Biomes vary from each other on the basis of type of the soil, amount of rainfall and temperature.

    ☐ True   ☐ False

22. The binomial system of nomenclature is also known as Linnaean system.

    ☐ True   ☐ False

23. According to the binomial system, the first name identifies the genus of the plant or the animal.

    ☐ True   ☐ False

24. The binomial system of nomenclature was devised by Charles Darwin.

    ☐ True   ☐ False

25. Adaptation plays an important role in evolution.

    ☐ True   ☐ False

26. Frogs are terricolous animals.

    ☐ True   ☐ False

27. Elephants are arboreal animals.
    ☐ True   ☐ False
28. Epiphytes do not harm the plants they grow on.
    ☐ True   ☐ False
29. Same animal may be a predator as well as a prey.
    ☐ True   ☐ False
30. Amphibians aestivate.
    ☐ True   ☐ False
31. Benthos is a type of bamboo plant.
    ☐ True   ☐ False
32. Planktons are small plants that grow at the bottom of the sea.
    ☐ True   ☐ False
33. Core is the outermost layer of the earth's surface.
    ☐ True   ☐ False
34. Fossils are important for our study of the history of life on earth.
    ☐ True   ☐ False

A Fossil

True & False

35. Paleontologists study the herd behaviour in animals.
    ☐ True   ☐ False

36. There has been more than one ice age on the earth.
    ☐ True   ☐ False

37. Sleeping is an example of biorhythm in animals.
    ☐ True   ☐ False

38. Dinosaurs belonged to the reptile family.
    ☐ True   ☐ False

39. There is an inexhaustible supply of coal available under the earth's surface.
    ☐ True   ☐ False

40. Most of the world's energy requirements are met with the help of nuclear power.
    ☐ True   ☐ False

41. Air has over 70% of nitrogen in it.
    ☐ True   ☐ False

42. The weight of the atmosphere is about 10.3 tonnes per square metre.
    ☐ True   ☐ False

43. Ozone is present in the stratosphere.
    ☐ True   ☐ False

44. Hydrogen is the main constituent of the exosphere.
    ☐ True   ☐ False

45. Infrared and radio waves coming from the sun are reflected back by the troposphere.
    ☐ True   ☐ False

46. Chemical fertilizers are always good for the environment.
    ☐ True   ☐ False

47. Only 47% of the sun's energy reaches the earth's surface.
    ☐ True   ☐ False
48. Aluminium is the most abundant element found in the earth's crust.
    ☐ True   ☐ False
49. Oxygen and hydrogen are two of the major constituents of seawater.
    ☐ True   ☐ False
50. Salamanders are amphibians.
    ☐ True   ☐ False
51. Plants and animals both breathe out carbon dioxide.
    ☐ True   ☐ False
52. Pesticides are poisonous and cause a threat to the environment.
    ☐ True   ☐ False
53. Pollution is mainly caused by human activities.
    ☐ True   ☐ False

Pesticides being sprayed into fields

True & False

54. Pollution destroys natural habitats and disturbs food chains and various cycles.
    ☐ True   ☐ False

55. Physical environment varies from time to time.
    ☐ True   ☐ False

56. Biomass is a renewable source of energy.
    ☐ True   ☐ False

57. Wind is a non-renewable source of energy.
    ☐ True   ☐ False

58. Approximately, one-third of the earth is considered to be under forest cover.
    ☐ True   ☐ False

59. The rate of forest loss is higher in tropical countries than in temperate ones.
    ☐ True   ☐ False

60. Forest cover can be increased by the practice of shift agriculture.
    ☐ True   ☐ False

61. Forest fires cause damage to forests and the wildlife.
    ☐ True   ☐ False

62. Loss of forest cover leads to soil erosion.
    ☐ True   ☐ False

63. Loss of forest cover increases the soil fertility.
    ☐ True   ☐ False

64. Every day, some species of plant or animal is becoming extinct somewhere on the earth.
    ☐ True   ☐ False

65. Oceans constitute about 90% of water on the earth.
    ☐ True   ☐ False

66. Vegetation cover is influenced by the climate.
    ☐ True   ☐ False
67. Climate of a region is affected by its vegetation.
    ☐ True   ☐ False
68. The storehouse of biodiversity is the rainforests.
    ☐ True   ☐ False
69. Terrace farming is practised in the plain regions.
    ☐ True   ☐ False
70. Soil erosion can be prevented by deforestation.
    ☐ True   ☐ False
71. Crop rotation causes soil erosion.
    ☐ True   ☐ False
72. An acid sulphate is a pollutant.
    ☐ True   ☐ False
73. Mining is beneficial to the environment.
    ☐ True   ☐ False
74. Drainage causes floods.
    ☐ True   ☐ False
75. A beetle is an example of omnivore.
    ☐ True   ☐ False
76. A frog is a herbivorous animal.
    ☐ True   ☐ False
77. Termites act as decomposers.
    ☐ True   ☐ False
78. Green plants are secondary producers.
    ☐ True   ☐ False
79. Herbivores are secondary producers.
    ☐ True   ☐ False

True & False

80. Herbivores are primary consumers.
    ☐ True   ☐ False
81. The organisms which directly eat green plants are called detritivores.
    ☐ True   ☐ False
82. Dead plant parts and animal remains are called detritus.
    ☐ True   ☐ False
83. Neem tree is used for treating skin ailments.
    ☐ True   ☐ False
84. India is the second largest country in the world.
    ☐ True   ☐ False
85. India is the second largest country in Asia.
    ☐ True   ☐ False
86. India is the seventh largest country in the world.
    ☐ True   ☐ False
87. The Trans-Himalayan region supports rare species like wild sheep and snow leopard.
    ☐ True   ☐ False
88. The Trans-Himalayan region supports endangered species, such as wolf and caracal.
    ☐ True   ☐ False
89. The desert zone supports endangered species, such as wolf, caracal and desert cat.
    ☐ True   ☐ False
90. Beta diversity refers to the number of species in a given area.
    ☐ True   ☐ False
91. Conservation of species can happen both on-site as well as off-site.
    ☐ True   ☐ False

A snow leopard

92. Oxides of nitrogen, sulphur and carbon are pollutants.

☐ **True**   ☐ **False**

93. Radioactivity can only occur in nature.

☐ **True**   ☐ **False**

94. Adsorption is a reversible process.

☐ **True**   ☐ **False**

95. RO is a technique of controlling noise pollution.

☐ **True**   ☐ **False**

96. Behavioural effect of noise pollution is the interference in the normal functioning of the body due to noise pollution.

☐ **True**   ☐ **False**

97. Cardiovascular problems are developed by noise pollution.

☐ **True**   ☐ **False**

98. Noise Pollution has no effect on human being's normal everyday sleep.

☐ True   ☐ False

99. Plutonium is not a radioactive element.

☐ True   ☐ False

100. Radioactivity is spontaneous disintegration of a nucleus.

☐ True   ☐ False

101. Television sets emit radiation.

☐ True   ☐ False

102. Haemoglobin has higher affinity to oxygen than carbon monoxide.

☐ True   ☐ False

103. The population when unchecked generally grows as arithmetic progression.

☐ True   ☐ False

104. Monoculture encourages biodiversity.

☐ True   ☐ False

105. The core of the earth is hot.

☐ True   ☐ False

106. Land degradation takes place only through natural causes.

☐ True   ☐ False

107. Crop rotation is one of the causes for soil erosion.

☐ True   ☐ False

108. Ecological pyramids were first devised by British ecologist Charles Elton.

☐ True   ☐ False

109. In a desert ecosystem, plants are not the primary producers.

☐ True   ☐ False

An anchialine cave

110. Anchialine caves are flooded caves.
     ☐ True   ☐ False

111. Biological diversity also helps in the formation and maintenance of soil.
     ☐ True   ☐ False

112. The root system prevents soil loss.
     ☐ True   ☐ False

113. The Indian rhinoceros is an extinct animal.
     ☐ True   ☐ False

114. The Blue Whale is an endangered species.
     ☐ True   ☐ False

115. Overhunting causes animal extinction.
     ☐ True   ☐ False

116. Tropical forests harbour maximum biodiversity in the world.
     ☐ True   ☐ False

117. Endemic species are only found in forests.
     ☐ True   ☐ False

True & False

118. Thermal pollution is the generation of large amounts of heat carried away as hot water into aquatic ecosystems.
    ☐ True   ☐ False

119. Cooling towers increase thermal pollution.
    ☐ True   ☐ False

120. Increased algae are an indication of water pollution.
    ☐ True   ☐ False

121. Mercury and lead are pollutants.
    ☐ True   ☐ False

122. Strip cropping and mulching are measures to prevent soil erosion.
    ☐ True   ☐ False

123. Clay soil retains more amount of water.
    ☐ True   ☐ False

124. Nuclear fission as well as fusion release enormous amount of energy.
    ☐ True   ☐ False

125. Tidal energy is produced from waves and tides.
    ☐ True   ☐ False

126. Fungi digest food outside their bodies.
    ☐ True   ☐ False

127. El Nino is a weather current that appears around December.
    ☐ True   ☐ False

128. More than 60 per cent of the Indian population depends on agriculture for its livelihood.
    ☐ True   ☐ False

129. The temperature of the world is decreasing every year.
    ☐ True   ☐ False

130. There are 14 biosphere reserves in India.
    ☐ True   ☐ False

131. The Nilgiri Biosphere Reserve was established in 1986.
    ☐ True   ☐ False

132. Alluvial soil is mostly found in river valleys.
    ☐ True   ☐ False

133. Saline soils are infertile.
    ☐ True   ☐ False

134. Peat soils are high in organic content.
    ☐ True   ☐ False

135. The Bhopal Gas Tragedy was a natural disaster.
    ☐ True   ☐ False

136. India has 16 per cent of the total human population.
    ☐ True   ☐ False

137. Conversion of tropical forests into farmlands eventually leads to soil erosion.
    ☐ True   ☐ False

138. Continental drifting is an example of natural change in the environment.
    ☐ True   ☐ False

139. Initially, all the continents were joined together in one big landmass.
    ☐ True   ☐ False

140. The continents have now stopped drifting.
    ☐ True   ☐ False

141. Tectonic plates are fixed in their places and cannot move.
    ☐ True   ☐ False

True & False

142. Earthquakes occur every day, but most of them are too low in magnitudes.
    ☐ **True**   ☐ **False**
143. There is only one solar system in the universe.
    ☐ **True**   ☐ **False**
144. The process of evolution continues to this day.
    ☐ **True**   ☐ **False**
145. The topmost layer of the soil shows maximum biological productivity.
    ☐ **True**   ☐ **False**
146. Ocean currents play an important role in determining climate patterns.
    ☐ **True**   ☐ **False**
147. The annual rate of continental drifting is 20 to 75 mm (approx.).
    ☐ **True**   ☐ **False**
148. Thunder is heard after the lightning is seen.
    ☐ **True**   ☐ **False**
149. Cyclones are frequent in tropical countries.
    ☐ **True**   ☐ **False**
150. The water under the earth's surface remains static.
    ☐ **True**   ☐ **False**
151. India is the second most populated country in the world.
    ☐ **True**   ☐ **False**
152. India has 16% of the world area.
    ☐ **True**   ☐ **False**
153. The gap between Food Grain Production and Population is decreasing with time.
    ☐ **True**   ☐ **False**

154. Only 15% (approx) area of the world can be used for agricultural purposes.
    ☐ True   ☐ False

155. Around 6 million hectares of farmland are disappearing every year due to various factors like housing, mines, roads, etc.
    ☐ True   ☐ False

156. Aerobic life forms are those forms which inhale carbon dioxide and exhale oxygen.
    ☐ True   ☐ False

157. Ozone protects us from the harmful ultraviolet rays of the sun.
    ☐ True   ☐ False

158. Continental drifting means that continents are slowly moving and are not stationary.
    ☐ True   ☐ False

159. The annual rate of continental drifting is 20 to 75 km (approx).
    ☐ True   ☐ False

160. Lightning occurs due to the negative charge carried by the clouds.
    ☐ True   ☐ False

161. Collision of Indian tectonic plate with the Asian tectonic plate gave rise to the Himalayas.
    ☐ True   ☐ False

162. The last ice age occurred millions of years ago.
    ☐ True   ☐ False

163. The last ice age ended around 3000 BC.
    ☐ True   ☐ False

True & False

164. Cyclone, hurricane and typhoon are all the same weather phenomenon with absolutely no difference.
   ☐ True   ☐ False

165. Cyclone, hurricane and typhoon are all the same weather phenomenon occurring at different regions and hence differ somewhat.
   ☐ True   ☐ False

166. Earthquakes have a very high frequency. There occur about 100 earthquakes per hour all around the world.
   ☐ True   ☐ False

167. The intensity of earthquakes can't be measured.
   ☐ True   ☐ False

168. The Richter Scale is used mainly to measure the intensity of earthquakes.
   ☐ True   ☐ False

169. Non-anthropogenic changes in the environment are actually man-made changes in the environment.
   ☐ True   ☐ False

170. Industrial Revolution started in 1840 in England.
   ☐ True   ☐ False

171. James Watt with his steam engine started the Industrial Revolution in 1780.
   ☐ True   ☐ False

172. Smog is smoke plus fog.
   ☐ True   ☐ False

173. Smog is basically a human-made change in the environment.
   ☐ True   ☐ False

174. An atom bomb was dropped on the USA by Japan in the World War I.
   ☐ True   ☐ False

A Steam Engine

175. Nagasaki and Hiroshima suffered heavy casualties due to atom bombs in the World War II.

    ☐ True   ☐ False

176. Atom bombs were dropped on August 6 and August 9, 1945 on Japan by the USA.

    ☐ True   ☐ False

177. The minamata disease is caused due to soil erosion.

    ☐ True   ☐ False

178. Intake of mercury causes the minamata disease.

    ☐ True   ☐ False

179. The Bhopal Gas Tragedy happened on the 3 December, 1984.

    ☐ True   ☐ False

180. The Bhopal Gas Tragedy (1984) happened due to a massive earthquake.

    ☐ True   ☐ False

181. The Iraq-USA war over the liberation of Kuwait had no effect on environment; it just caused loss of human lives.
☐ True   ☐ False

182. India has the lowest literacy rate in the world.
☐ True   ☐ False

183. India has the largest number of malnourished people.
☐ True   ☐ False

184. India is the most populated country in the world.
☐ True   ☐ False

185. Developed countries only have 16% of the world population and they consume 60% of the total food and 70% of the total energy generated.
☐ True   ☐ False

186. Developing countries are responsible for maximum environmental degradation.
☐ True   ☐ False

187. Approximately 99% of our food is contaminated with pesticides.
☐ True   ☐ False

188. Within the next 30 years, about 25% of the world species will risk extinction.
☐ True   ☐ False

189. In the Bhopal Gas Tragedy, the gas leaked was methyl isocyanate.
☐ True   ☐ False

190. Approximately the Big Bang started around 100 billion years ago.
☐ True   ☐ False

191. The Sun is around 150 million km away from the earth.
☐ True   ☐ False

192. One light year is the distance travelled by the light in one earth year.

☐ True   ☐ False

193. The Sun is actually a big fusion reactor.

☐ True   ☐ False

194. Neon is the most abundant element on the earth.

☐ True   ☐ False

195. Approximately life forms began around 3.5 billion years ago.

☐ True   ☐ False

196. Lithosphere is the earth's crust made of the mantle of rocks.

☐ True   ☐ False

197. Soil forms due to the continuous degradation of rocks.

☐ True   ☐ False

198. A typical soil consists of around 95% organic matter and 5% of inorganic matter.

☐ True   ☐ False

199. The top soil is most productive for agricultural purposes.

☐ True   ☐ False

200. Deforestation doesn't affect the top soil.

☐ True   ☐ False

201. Sound energy is transferred through compressions and rarefactions.

☐ True   ☐ False

202. Sounds in the frequency range of 4000 to 20,000 Hz cause most of the damage to the nerve fibres in humans.

☐ True   ☐ False

203. The unit used to measure sound is called Hertz, with the symbol Hz

☐ True   ☐ False

204. The ability to hear increases with age.
    ☐ True   ☐ False

205. In mammals, the ability to hear is at its peak at the time of birth.
    ☐ True   ☐ False

206. Noise pollution is defined as the sounds/noises that are harmful as well as annoying.
    ☐ True   ☐ False

207. When sound enters the ear, it is transferred to the brain as a nerve impulse.
    ☐ True   ☐ False

208. Human-induced noises interfere with the sounds of hunting, navigating and communicating used by the marine animals.
    ☐ True   ☐ False

209. Humans are born with a hearing range of 16 to 30,000 Hz.
    ☐ True   ☐ False

210. Natural processes by which pollutants are removed from a medium are called *sinks*.
    ☐ True   ☐ False

211. Methanol and ethanol are cleaner and more environment-friendly than petroleum-based fuels.
    ☐ True   ☐ False

212. Biogas is produced by the biological breakdown of organic matter.
    ☐ True   ☐ False

213. Biogas and natural gas can be compressed.
    ☐ True   ☐ False

A biogas plant

214. Anaerobic digestion is the process of breaking down biodegradable materials to produce energy.

☐ True ☐ False

215. Anaerobic digestion takes place in the presence of oxygen.

☐ True ☐ False

216. Anaerobic digestion can also be done for a few non-biodegradable materials.

☐ True ☐ False

217. Sewage sludge is also used for producing biogas.

☐ True ☐ False

218. Natural gas is produced by nuclear fusion.

☐ True ☐ False

219. Natural gas is mainly methane.

☐ True ☐ False

220. Natural gas is a fossil fuel.

☐ True ☐ False

True & False

221. Fossil fuels are renewable resources.
☐ True   ☐ False

222. Mining facilitates sustainable development.
☐ True   ☐ False

223. Surface mining is more common than underground or sub-surface mining.
☐ True   ☐ False

224. Tailings are waste generated by ore mills.
☐ True   ☐ False

225. Mining can also create *sinkholes*.
☐ True   ☐ False

226. The Silicosis disease occurs due to constant exposure to the crystalline silica dust.
☐ True   ☐ False

227. Vector-borne diseases are caused by the bite of certain infected arthropods.
☐ True   ☐ False

228. Arthropods are warm-blooded organisms.
☐ True   ☐ False

229. In water-borne diseases, water acts as the medium for the diseases to spread.
☐ True   ☐ False

230. Excess fluoride is good for the teeth.
☐ True   ☐ False

231. pH is used for measuring the number of hydrogen ions in a given solution.
☐ True   ☐ False

232. The pH of water is 7, hence it is acidic in nature.
☐ True   ☐ False

233. Gases contract when heated.
    ☐ True   ☐ False

234. Warm air moves up in the atmosphere.
    ☐ True   ☐ False

235. Temperature increases with altitude.
    ☐ True   ☐ False

236. Everglades is a biologically diverse wetland situated in Florida.
    ☐ True   ☐ False

237. Pulp is the raw material produced from trees used for making paper.
    ☐ True   ☐ False

238. Strip mining is an environment-friendly method of extracting minerals from the earth.
    ☐ True   ☐ False

239. A pass is a route through a mountain or a ridge.
    ☐ True   ☐ False

240. High humus content is an indication of fertility of the soil.
    ☐ True   ☐ False

241. Rapids are characterised by low currents.
    ☐ True   ☐ False

242. Backwater is characterised by swift flowing water.
    ☐ True   ☐ False

243. A subcontinent is bigger than a continent.
    ☐ True   ☐ False

244. A subcontinent is a part of a continent.
    ☐ True   ☐ False

245. A body of water surrounded entirely by land is called an island.
    ☐ True   ☐ False

246. A body of water surrounded entirely by land is called a lake.
     ☐ True   ☐ False

247. The island groups of Andaman and Nicobar are located in the Bay of Bengal.
     ☐ True   ☐ False

248. Lakshadweep is located in the Bay of Bengal.
     ☐ True   ☐ False

249. Lakshadweep is located in the Arabian Sea.
     ☐ True   ☐ False

250. Karewas are thick deposits of glacial clay.
     ☐ True   ☐ False

251. Karewas are conducive for the cultivation of zafran or saffron.
     ☐ True   ☐ False

252. The Kashmir Himalayas are famous for karewa formations.
     ☐ True   ☐ False

253. The Dal Lake is a saltwater lake.
     ☐ True   ☐ False

254. Jhelum and Chenab are tributaries of River Indus.
     ☐ True   ☐ False

255. Jhelum forms meanders in Srinagar.
     ☐ True   ☐ False

256. A strait is a navigable channel of water that connects two larger bodies of water.
     ☐ True   ☐ False

257. The IAEA was established in 1957.
     ☐ True   ☐ False

258. A bay is a body of water completely surrounded by land.
     ☐ True   ☐ False

259. Some coves can also be called bays.
☐ **True**   ☐ **False**

260. A fjord is a narrow inlet with steep cliffs on both sides.
☐ **True**   ☐ **False**

261. A fjord is formed by glacial activity.
☐ **True**   ☐ **False**

262. The catchments of small rivers are called watersheds.
☐ **True**   ☐ **False**

263. The Chenab is the largest tributary of River Indus.
☐ **True**   ☐ **False**

264. The Mahananda is a tributary of River Brahmaputra.
☐ **True**   ☐ **False**

265. A lagoon is a body of sea water separated by the sea by some barrier.
☐ **True**   ☐ **False**

266. Landfills are environment-friendly method of waste disposal.
☐ **True**   ☐ **False**

267. The International Atomic Energy Agency (IAEA) is an international agency that advocates peaceful use of nuclear energy.
☐ **True**   ☐ **False**

268. The IAEA was established in 1986.
☐ **True**   ☐ **False**

269. A gulf is a kind of bay.
☐ **True**   ☐ **False**

270. Fukushima nuclear disaster took place after the Tohoku earthquake in Japan.
☐ **True**   ☐ **False**

271. Weather changes more frequently than climate.
    ☐ True   ☐ False

272. Tropical deciduous forests can further be divided into dry and moist deciduous forests.
    ☐ True   ☐ False

273. Cholera is a type of lung infection.
    ☐ True   ☐ False

274. Cholera is an infection in the small intestine.
    ☐ True   ☐ False

275. Cholera is caused by a virus.
    ☐ True   ☐ False

276. Cholera is caused by a bacteria.
    ☐ True   ☐ False

277. In India, the Project Tiger was implemented in 1973.
    ☐ True   ☐ False

278. Excess water in plants is transpired via stomata.
    ☐ True   ☐ False

279. Stomata in plants are found in the roots.
    ☐ True   ☐ False

280. Stomata in plants are located on the leaf and stem.
    ☐ True   ☐ False

281. Transpiration is to plants what sweating is to humans.
    ☐ True   ☐ False

282. A photometer is used to measure the uptake of water.
    ☐ True   ☐ False

283. The moon was formed before the earth.
    ☐ True   ☐ False

284. Red stars are stars that have exhausted their supply of hydrogen atoms.
    ☐ True   ☐ False

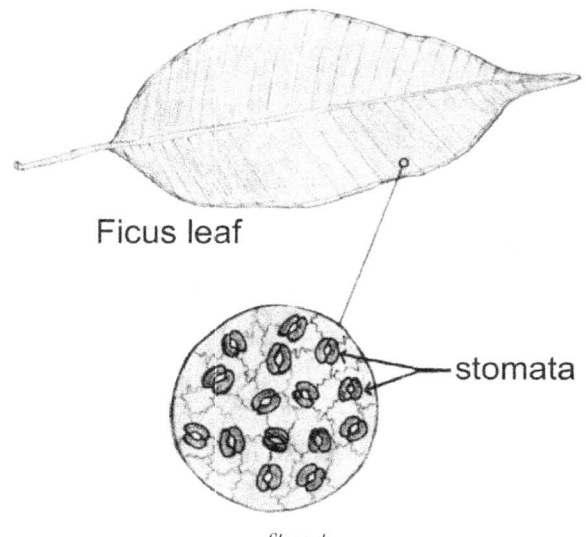

Ficus leaf

stomata

Stomata

285. Roots of a plant can also be aerial.
    ☐ True   ☐ False

286. Rhizomes are underground stems.
    ☐ True   ☐ False

287. Ginger is a type of rhizome used directly by humans.
    ☐ True   ☐ False

288. Radicle is the first root of a plant.
    ☐ True   ☐ False

289. A carrot is an example of storage roots.
    ☐ True   ☐ False

290. A beet is an example of tuberous roots.
    ☐ True   ☐ False

291. Figs are commonly found in rainforest ecosystems.
    ☐ True   ☐ False

True & False

292. Roots bind the soil and prevent soil erosion.
    ☐ True   ☐ False
293. A dune is a hill of sand built by wind.
    ☐ True   ☐ False
294. Ergs are broad and wide areas covered mostly with sand.
    ☐ True   ☐ False
295. Ergs are conducive to all forms of vegetation.
    ☐ True   ☐ False
296. The Sahara Desert is the largest hot desert in the world.
    ☐ True   ☐ False
297. A depression is a sunken landform below the surrounding area.
    ☐ True   ☐ False
298. A salt storm is a phenomenon most frequent around the Aral Sea.
    ☐ True   ☐ False
299. When the soil salinity is high, the soil is more fertile.
    ☐ True   ☐ False
300. The Laterite soil is formed by leaching.
    ☐ True   ☐ False

Answers

1.	False	24.	False	47.	True	70.	False
2.	False	25.	True	48.	False	71.	False
3.	True	26.	False	49.	True	72.	True
4.	True	27.	False	50.	True	73.	False
5.	True	28.	True	51.	True	74.	False
6.	True	29.	True	52.	True	75.	False
7.	True	30.	False	53.	True	76.	False
8.	False	31.	False	54.	True	77.	False
9.	True	32.	False	55.	True	78.	False
10.	False	33.	False	56.	True	79.	False
11.	True	34.	True	57.	False	80.	True
12.	True	35.	False	58.	True	81.	False
13.	True	36.	True	59.	True	82.	True
14.	True	37.	True	60.	False	83.	True
15.	False	38.	True	61.	True	84.	False
16.	True	39.	False	62.	True	85.	True
17.	True	40.	False	63.	False	86.	True
18.	True	41.	True	64.	True	87.	True
19.	False	42.	True	65.	True	88.	False
20.	False	43.	True	66.	True	89.	True
21.	True	44.	True	67.	True	90.	False
22.	True	45.	True	68.	True	91.	True
23.	True	46.	False	69.	False	92.	True

True & False

93. False	121. True	149. True	177. False
94. True	122. True	150. False	178. True
95. False	123. True	151. True	179. True
96. False	124. True	152. False	180. False
97. True	125. True	153. False	181. False
98. False	126. True	154. True	182. True
99. False	127. True	155. True	183. True
100. True	128. True	156. False	184. False
101. True	129. False	157. True	185. True
102. False	130. True	158. True	186. False
103. False	131. True	159. False	187. False
104. False	132. True	160. True	188. True
105. True	133. True	161. True	189. True
106. False	134. True	162. False	190. False
107. False	135. False	163. True	191. True
108. True	136. True	164. False	192. True
109. False	137. True	165. True	193. True
110. True	138. True	166. True	194. False
111. True	139. True	167. False	195. True
112. True	140. False	168. True	196. True
113. False	141. False	169. False	197. True
114. True	142. True	170. False	198. False
115. True	143. False	171. True	199. True
116. True	144. True	172. True	200. False
117. False	145. True	173. True	201. True
118. True	146. True	174. False	202. True
119. False	147. True	175. True	203. True
120. True	148. True	176. True	204. False

205. True	229. True	253. False	277. True
206. True	230. False	254. True	278. True
207. True	231. True	255. True	279. False
208. True	232. False	256. True	280. True
209. True	233. False	257. True	281. True
210. True	234. True	258. False	282. True
211. True	235. False	259. True	283. False
212. True	236. True	260. True	284. True
213. True	237. True	261. True	285. True
214. True	238. False	262. True	286. True
215. False	239. True	263. True	287. True
216. False	240. True	264. False	288. True
217. True	241. False	265. True	289. True
218. False	242. False	266. False	290. False
219. True	243. False	267. True	291. True
220. True	244. True	268. False	292. True
221. False	245. False	269. True	293. True
222. False	246. True	270. True	294. True
223. True	247. True	271. True	295. False
224. True	248. False	272. True	296. True
225. True	249. True	273. False	297. True
226. True	250. True	274. True	298. True
227. True	251. True	275. False	299. False
228. False	252. True	276. True	300. True

MULTIPLE CHOICE QUESTIONS (MCQs)

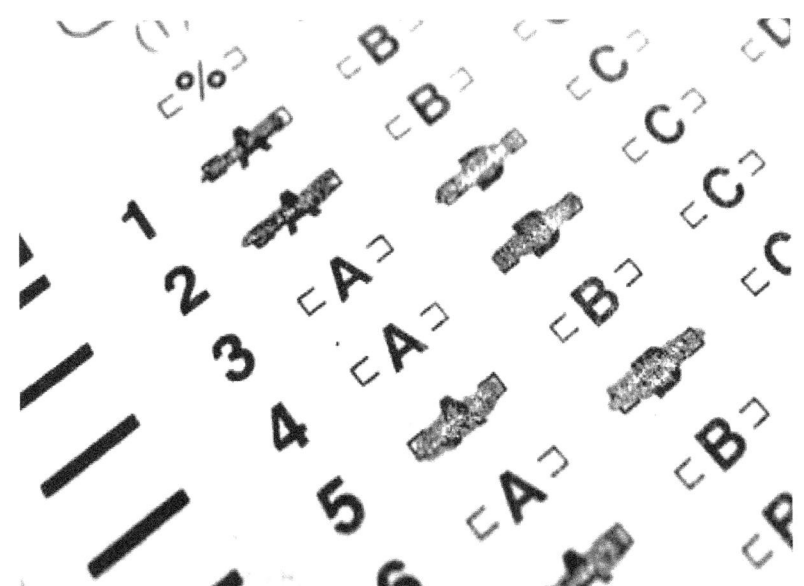

Multiple Choice Questions

MCQ-1. Which of the following chemicals is present in acid rain?

- **ⓐ** Sulphuric acid
- **ⓑ** Paraffin wax
- **ⓒ** Carbon dioxide
- **ⓓ** Aluminium

MCQ-2. Which of the following substances is non-biodegradable?

- **ⓐ** Plastic
- **ⓑ** Manure
- **ⓒ** Paper
- **ⓓ** Wood

MCQ-3. The Kaziranga Sanctuary is located in:

- **ⓐ** Lucknow
- **ⓑ** Bhopal
- **ⓒ** Manipur
- **ⓓ** Assam

MCQ-4. El Nino is the name of:

- **ⓐ** An extinct animal
- **ⓑ** A motor vehicle
- **ⓒ** A weather current
- **ⓓ** A hurricane

MCQ-5. Which of the following is not an Indian biosphere reserve?

- **ⓐ** Sunderbans
- **ⓑ** Nilgiri
- **ⓒ** Gulf of Mannar
- **ⓓ** Gulf of Kachh

MCQ-6. The Sandalwood tree can be found in a/an:

- **ⓐ** Deciduous forest
- **ⓑ** Deltaic forest
- **ⓒ** Evergreen forest
- **ⓓ** Thorny forest

MCQ-7. The Alluvial soil is deposited by:

- **ⓐ** Rivers and streams
- **ⓑ** Wind
- **ⓒ** Rain
- **ⓓ** Living organisms

Multiple Choice Questions (MCQs)

A deciduous forest cover

MCQ-8. Black soil lacks:
- **a** Iron
- **b** Phosphorus
- **c** Magnesia
- **d** Alumina

MCQ-9. Arid soil is:
- **a** Red or brown in colour
- **b** Yellow in colour
- **c** Deep grey in colour
- **d** Black in colour

MCQ-10. Which of the following gases was mainly responsible for the Bhopal Gas Tragedy?
- **a** Methyl isocyanate
- **b** Methane
- **c** Sulphur dioxide
- **d** Carbon dioxide

MCQ-11. The Bhopal Gas Tragedy took place on:
- **a** December 3, 1984
- **b** October 5, 1996
- **c** December 3, 1996
- **d** October 5, 1984

MCQ-12. In which gas plant did the Bhopal Gas Tragedy take place?
- **a** Hindustan Mint and Agro Products
- **b** Union Carbide (India) Ltd
- **c** Pacific Agricorp Pvt Ltd
- **d** Dow Chemical Co

MCQ-13. The annual rate of continent drifting is:
- ⓐ 15 to 16 cm
- ⓑ 17 to 18 inches
- ⓒ 20 to 75 mm
- ⓓ 1 to 2 km

MCQ-14. The last Ice Age took place:
- ⓐ 200 million years ago
- ⓑ 1500 years ago
- ⓒ 18,000 years ago.
- ⓓ 16 million years ago

MCQ-15. Earthquakes take place due to:
- ⓐ Movement in tectonic plates
- ⓑ Global warming
- ⓒ Habitat destruction
- ⓓ Change in weather

MCQ-16. The Earth's outer crust is divided into:
- ⓐ Seven large tectonic plates
- ⓑ 16 large tectonic tectonic plates
- ⓒ Two tectonic plates
- ⓓ Innumerable plates

MCQ-17. During a shift/collision in the tectonic plates, the energy is released in the form of:
- ⓐ Radiation
- ⓑ Sound waves
- ⓒ Seismic waves
- ⓓ Ultraviolet radiation

MCQ-18. The intensity of an earthquake is measured on a :
- ⓐ Richter scale
- ⓑ Speedometer
- ⓒ Ammeter
- ⓓ Volt meter

MCQ-19. Who said these words: "Poverty is the worst form of pollution..."
- ⓐ Rajiv Gandhi
- ⓑ Jawaharlal Nehru
- ⓒ Indira Gandhi
- ⓓ Mahatma Gandhi

Multiple Choice Questions (MCQs)

MCQ-20. The Big Bang is a theory about:
- **a** A car accident
- **c** The beginning of the universe
- **b** A nuclear radiation leak
- **d** An atomic bomb explosion

MCQ-21. A light year is a unit used to measure:
- **a** Radiation
- **c** Time
- **b** Brightness
- **d** Distance

MCQ-22. The closest star to the earth is:
- **a** Mercury
- **c** Sun
- **b** Moon
- **d** Pluto

MCQ-23. Ocean basins are made of:
- **a** Basaltic rock
- **c** Silicates
- **b** Granite rock
- **d** Phosphates

MCQ-24. The landmass of the earth (continents) is made up of:
- **a** Basaltic rock
- **c** Silicates
- **b** Granite rock
- **d** Phosphates

MCQ-25. Granite rocks are made of:
- **a** Calcium sulphate
- **c** Aluminium silicate
- **b** Sodium chloride
- **d** Phosphates

MCQ-26. Basaltic rocks are made of:
- **a** Calcium sulphate
- **c** Aluminium phosphate
- **b** Magnesium silicate
- **d** Aluminium silicate

MCQ-27. The first life form to appear on the earth was:
- **a** Man
- **c** Cactus plant
- **b** Dinosaur
- **d** Blue-green algae

MCQ-28. How many layers does soil have?
    ⓐ One   **ⓒ** Three
    ⓑ Two   **ⓓ** Four

MCQ-29. Hydrosphere does not consist of:
    ⓐ Oceans   **ⓒ** Glaciers
    ⓑ Rainwater   **ⓓ** Lakes

MCQ-30. The carbon dioxide level in the atmosphere is directly related to:
    ⓐ The earth's   **ⓒ** Water scarcity
       temperature
    ⓑ The type of   **ⓓ** Soil erosion
       vegetation

MCQ-31. Lightning during rains is a form of:
    ⓐ Thunder   **ⓒ** Sound release
    ⓑ Electric discharge   **ⓓ** Bright clouds

MCQ-32. The speed of light is:
    ⓐ Faster than the speed   **ⓒ** One-eighth the
       of sound   speed of sound
    ⓑ Slower than the   **ⓓ** Equal to the speed
       speed of sound   of sound

MCQ-33. Blue-agree algae appeared:
    ⓐ On the landmass   **ⓒ** Around trees
    ⓑ In the atmosphere   **ⓓ** On the surface of
                                the ocean

MCQ-34. The last living organism to appear on earth was:
    ⓐ Blue whale   **ⓒ** Humans
    ⓑ Dolphin   **ⓓ** Birds

Multiple Choice Questions (MCQs)

MCQ-35. The geological cycle means:
- ⓐ Recycling of the earth's crust
- ⓑ Change in the geographical features of a region
- ⓒ The constant movement of carbon in the atmosphere
- ⓓ The constant movement of living beings from one place to another

MCQ-36. Plants give off excess water through the process of:
- ⓐ Respiration
- ⓑ Transpiration
- ⓒ Evaporation
- ⓓ Condensation

MCQ-37. One major cause of eutrophication is:
- ⓐ Phosphate pollution of water
- ⓑ Chlorine pollution of water
- ⓒ Excess carbon in water
- ⓓ Sulphate pollution in water

MCQ-38. Rocks formed after cooling of molten lava are called:
- ⓐ Granite rocks
- ⓑ Igneous rocks
- ⓒ Sedimentary rocks
- ⓓ Glaciers

Igneous rock

MCQ-39. The Tundra biome is in the:
- **ⓐ** Tropical region
- **ⓒ** Polar region
- **ⓑ** Equatorial region
- **ⓓ** Desert region

MCQ-40. Pine trees are found in:
- **ⓐ** Deciduous forests
- **ⓒ** Deserts
- **ⓑ** Coniferous forests
- **ⓓ** Polar region

MCQ-41. Tropical rainforests are found near the:
- **ⓐ** Equator
- **ⓒ** South Pole
- **ⓑ** North Pole
- **ⓓ** Desert region

MCQ-42. Marine water has high amount of:
- **ⓐ** Phosphates
- **ⓒ** Salt
- **ⓑ** Carbon
- **ⓓ** Nitrates

MCQ-43. Mangroves are:
- **ⓐ** A variety of mangoes
- **ⓒ** A variety of fish food
- **ⓑ** Forests found between land and sea
- **ⓓ** None of these

MCQ-44. The habitat of the Royal Bengal Tiger is:
- **ⓐ** The Sahara Desert
- **ⓒ** The Sunderbans
- **ⓑ** The Kaziranga National Park
- **ⓓ** None of these

MCQ-45. In India, forests are mainly cut down for:
- **ⓐ** Firewood (fuel)
- **ⓒ** Furniture industry
- **ⓑ** Paper making
- **ⓓ** Timber

MCQ-46. Which of the following is not a freshwater ecosystem?
- **ⓐ** Ponds
- **ⓒ** Springs
- **ⓑ** Lakes
- **ⓓ** Seas

Multiple Choice Questions (MCQs)

A tiger in the Sunderbans

MCQ-47. Green plants make their own food, hence they are:
- ⓐ Autotrophic
- ⓑ Heterotrophic
- ⓒ Consumers
- ⓓ Secondary consumers

MCQ-48. Which of the following elements is common in all the ecosystems on the earth?
- ⓐ The sun
- ⓑ The moon
- ⓒ Soil
- ⓓ Man

MCQ-49. Transpiration is a phenomenon that takes place in:
- ⓐ Birds
- ⓑ Plants
- ⓒ Aquatic animals
- ⓓ Humans

MCQ-50. Human beings first appeared on earth:
- ⓐ 3.5 billion years ago
- ⓑ 5 million years ago
- ⓒ 1 billion years ago
- ⓓ In 3000 B C

MCQ-51. When human-induced activities produce noise that interfere with marine mammals' communication, navigation, etc., the phenomenon is called:

ⓐ Noise pollution   ⓒ Marine pollution

ⓑ Noise trauma   ⓓ Masking

MCQ-52. Which of the following is not an example of noise pollution?

ⓐ Masking   ⓒ Blast trauma

ⓑ Noise trauma   ⓓ Deforestation

MCQ-53. For which of the following does the Doppler Effect not apply to?

ⓐ Sound waves   ⓒ Electromagnetic waves

ⓑ Water ripples   ⓓ Carbon dating

MCQ-54. Which of the following produces the loudest noise?

ⓐ A dog barking   ⓒ A jet plane taking off

ⓑ A vacuum cleaner   ⓓ A chain saw

MCQ-55. Which of the following is the time period required for a country's population to grow double?

ⓐ Fertility rate   ⓒ Light year

ⓑ Mortality rate   ⓓ Doubling time

MCQ-56. Overpopulation directly affects the:

ⓐ Carrying capacity of a region   ⓒ Ozone layer

ⓑ Pollution   ⓓ Noise pollution

MCQ-57. Pedology is the study of:

ⓐ Feet   ⓒ Soil

ⓑ Children diet   ⓓ Forest cover

Multiple Choice Questions (MCQs)

MCQ-58. Leaching helps in:
- **ⓐ** Soil formation
- **ⓒ** Transpiration
- **ⓑ** Continent drifting
- **ⓓ** Photosynthesis

MCQ-59. Offensive odours produced by small or big-scale industries have given rise to:
- **ⓐ** Odour pollution
- **ⓒ** Body odour
- **ⓑ** Bad breath
- **ⓓ** None of these

MCQ-60. Which of the following gases is not present in biogas?
- **ⓐ** Methane
- **ⓒ** Sulphur dioxide
- **ⓑ** Carbon dioxide
- **ⓓ** Hydrogen sulphide

MCQ-61. Which of the following cannot be used to produce biogas?
- **ⓐ** Manure
- **ⓒ** Plastic bottles
- **ⓑ** Kitchen waste
- **ⓓ** Decayed plants

MCQ-62. A mix of gases produced within a landfill due to the action of certain microorganisms is called:
- **ⓐ** Greenhouse gas
- **ⓒ** Landfill gas
- **ⓑ** Methane
- **ⓓ** None of these

MCQ-63. Which of the following is not a fossil fuel?
- **ⓐ** Coal
- **ⓒ** Biogas
- **ⓑ** Petroleum
- **ⓓ** Natural gas

MCQ-64. Sandstone turns into _____ through tectonic compression and heating.
- **ⓐ** Quartzite rock
- **ⓒ** Charcoal
- **ⓑ** Quartz
- **ⓓ** Opal

MCQ-65. Which of the following is not a mining-related disease?
- **ⓐ** AIDS
- **ⓑ** Silicosis
- **ⓒ** Pneumoconiosis
- **ⓓ** Asbestosis

MCQ-66. Which of the following is also known as miner's lung disease?
- **ⓐ** Silicosis
- **ⓑ** Pneumoconiosis
- **ⓒ** Asbestosis
- **ⓓ** None of these

MCQ-67. Old, abandoned mines which have no oxygen are called:
- **ⓐ** Canyons
- **ⓑ** Caves
- **ⓒ** Blackdamp
- **ⓓ** Sinkholes

MCQ-68. Which disease is also known as Potter's rot?
- **ⓐ** Silicosis
- **ⓑ** Asbestosis
- **ⓒ** Pneumoconiosis
- **ⓓ** None of these

MCQ-69. Which of the following is not a carrier of vector-borne diseases?
- **ⓐ** Mosquito
- **ⓑ** Bugs
- **ⓒ** Ticks
- **ⓓ** Butterflies

MCQ-70. The scientific study of climate patterns is called:
- **ⓐ** Limnology
- **ⓑ** Meteorology
- **ⓒ** Climatology
- **ⓓ** Ethology

MCQ-71. Which of the following is not a type of precipitation?
- **ⓐ** Rain
- **ⓑ** Hail
- **ⓒ** Snow
- **ⓓ** Wind

Multiple Choice Questions (MCQs)

MCQ-72. What is the measure of acidity or basicity of an aqueous solution?
  - **a** pH
  - **b** Decibel
  - **c** Frequency
  - **d** Wave length

MCQ-73. What is the pH of water?
  - **a** 7
  - **b** 8.5
  - **c** 16
  - **d** 1

MCQ-74. The rate at which temperature drops with the increase in altitude is called:
  - **a** Global warming
  - **b** Atmospheric pressure
  - **c** Environmental Lapse Rate (ELR)
  - **d** None of these

MCQ-75. An underground source of water is called:
  - **a** Stream
  - **b** Lake
  - **c** Aquifer
  - **d** Canal

MCQ-76. Substances that cause cancer in living beings are called:
  - **a** Pollutants
  - **b** CFCs
  - **c** Carcinogens
  - **d** None of these

MCQ-77. A legal limit imposed on countries or companies regarding the amount of greenhouse gas emission is called:
  - **a** Emission cap
  - **b** Kyoto Protocol
  - **c** International treaty
  - **d** None of these

MCQ-78. A bay at the mouth of a water body in which large quantities of freshwater and seawater mix together is called:
  - **a** A gulf
  - **b** A coral reef
  - **c** An estuary
  - **d** An island

An estuary

MCQ-79. The study of genes and hereditary characteristics among humans is called:
- ⓐ Ecology
- ⓒ Eugenics
- ⓑ Evolution
- ⓓ None of these

MCQ-80. The depletion of dissolved oxygen in water is called:
- ⓐ Anorexia
- ⓒ Hydroxia
- ⓑ Hypoxia
- ⓓ None of these

MCQ-81. Leukaemia is:
- ⓐ A form of bone marrow cancer
- ⓒ A type of cyclone
- ⓑ A food disorder
- ⓓ None of these

MCQ-82. The study of oceans and ocean life is called:
- ⓐ Oceanography
- ⓒ Ecology
- ⓑ Hydrology
- ⓓ Limnology

Multiple Choice Questions (MCQs)

MCQ-83. Fish that live at or near the water surface are called:
- ⓐ Benthos
- ⓑ Pelagic
- ⓒ Demersal
- ⓓ Groundfish

MCQ-84. Which of the following is not a radioactive element?
- ⓐ Plutonium
- ⓑ Sodium
- ⓒ Uranium
- ⓓ Radium

MCQ-85. Radon is:
- ⓐ A radioactive element
- ⓑ A radioactive gas
- ⓒ A radar system
- ⓓ None of these

MCQ-86. A region over which water flows into a river, stream or reservoir is called:
- ⓐ Dam
- ⓑ Tributary
- ⓒ Estuary
- ⓓ Watershed

MCQ-87. A group of islands that lie close together is called:
- ⓐ Continent
- ⓑ Archipelago
- ⓒ Bunding
- ⓓ None of these

MCQ-88. A stretch of water that has been bypassed by the main flow of a stream but is still connected to it is called a:
- ⓐ Stream
- ⓑ Tributary
- ⓒ Backwater
- ⓓ Bay

MCQ-89. When embankments are constructed around crop fields to conserve water and soil, the practice is called:
- ⓐ Soil conservation
- ⓑ Dam building
- ⓒ Watershed management
- ⓓ Bunding

An archipelago

MCQ-90. Small marine polyps that occur in colonies found in warm shallow sea water are called:
- **a** Coral
- **c** Plankton
- **b** Reef
- **d** None of these

MCQ-91. The area drained by a major river or its tributaries is called a/an:
- **a** Bay
- **c** Catchment area
- **b** Estuary
- **d** Embankment

MCQ-92. A grained metamorphic rock with a banded structure that is formed during mountain building or volcanic activity is called:
- **a** Igneous rock
- **c** Gneiss
- **b** Granite rock
- **d** None of these

Multiple Choice Questions (MCQs)

MCQ-93. A deep valley with steep and rocky side walls is called a:
- ⓐ Mountain
- ⓑ Plateau
- ⓒ Gorge
- ⓓ None of these

MCQ-94. The dead organic content of the soil which increases its fertility is called:
- ⓐ Humus
- ⓑ Fossils
- ⓒ Terricolous animals
- ⓓ None of these

MCQ-95. A piece of land jutting out into the sea is called:
- ⓐ An estuary
- ⓑ An island
- ⓒ A bay
- ⓓ A peninsula

MCQ-96. An area which is reserved for the conservation of animals is called:
- ⓐ Zoo
- ⓑ Sanctuary
- ⓒ Forests
- ⓓ None of these

MCQ-97. The layer of solid rocks at the bottom of the three sub-layers of soil is called:
- ⓐ Sub-soil
- ⓑ Top soil
- ⓒ Bedrock
- ⓓ None of these

MCQ-98. A mass of snow and ice that slowly moves away from its place of formation is called:
- ⓐ Glacier
- ⓑ Mountain
- ⓒ Island
- ⓓ None of these

MCQ-99. An enormous mass of ice that floats on big water bodies, with only a small portion of it visible above the water surface is called:
- ⓐ Glacier
- ⓑ Iceberg
- ⓒ Mountain
- ⓓ None of these

MCQ-100.   A mass of land that is surrounded by water on all sides, and is smaller in size than a continent is called:

    a Gully   **c** Bay

    b Island   **d** Gulf

Multiple Choice Questions (MCQs)

Answers

(1) a	(23) a	(45) a	(67) c
(2) a	(24) b	(46) d	(68) a
(3) d	(25) c	(47) a	(69) d
(4) c	(26) b	(48) a	(70) c
(5) d	(27) d	(49) b	(71) d
(6) a	(28) c	(50) b	(72) a
(7) a	(29) b	(51) d	(73) a
(8) b	(30) a	(52) d	(74) c
(9) a	(31) b	(53) d	(75) c
(10) a	(32) a	(54) c	(76) c
(11) a	(33) d	(55) d	(77) a
(12) b	(34) c	(56) a	(78) c
(13) c	(35) a	(57) c	(79) c
(14) c	(36) b	(58) a	(80) b
(15) a	(37) a	(59) a	(81) a
(16) a	(38) b	(60) c	(82) a
(17) c	(39) c	(61) c	(83) b
(18) a	(40) b	(62) c	(84) b
(19) c	(41) a	(63) c	(85) b
(20) c	(42) c	(64) a	(86) d
(21) d	(43) b	(65) a	(87) b
(22) c	(44) c	(66) b	(88) c

(89) **d**	(92) **c**	(95) **d**	(98) **a**
(90) **a**	(93) **c**	(96) **b**	(99) **b**
(91) **c**	(94) **a**	(97) **c**	(100) **b**

WORD SEARCH

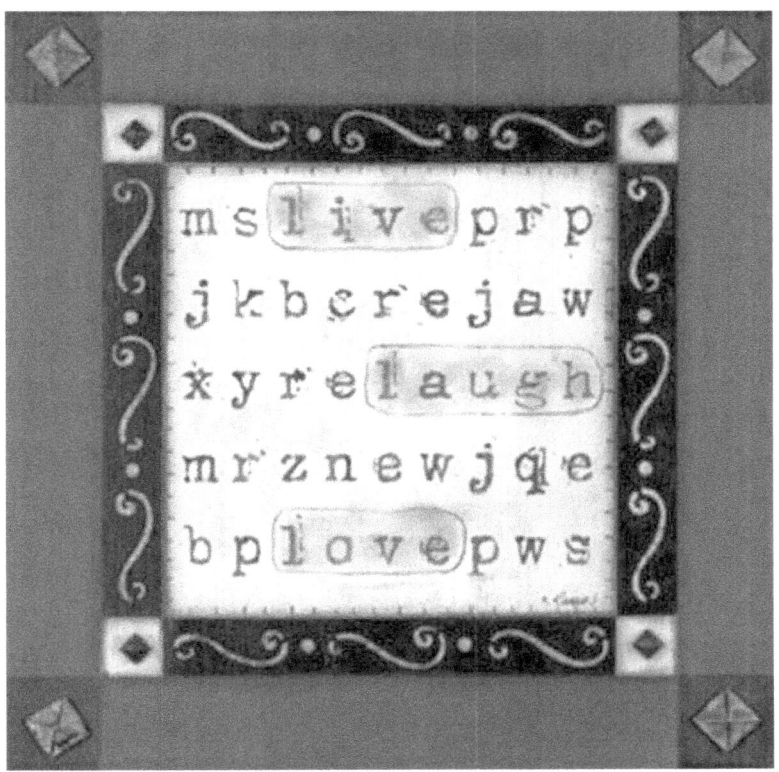

T	E	D	I	L	T	G	M	L	G	N	I	H	C	A	O	P
P	B	O	L	O	P	E	S	N	S	A	V	A	N	N	A	T
P	E	E	G	O	R	I	S	A	N	O	M	T	U	G	Y	V
O	O	N	B	C	L	O	Y	U	O	O	M	T	G	N	G	N
T	M	T	U	I	M	E	G	H	U	L	T	C	Q	O	O	D
N	S	R	C	J	Y	U	O	F	Y	H	S	U	M	I	L	O
O	Y	O	E	R	H	G	L	G	Y	U	I	S	T	S	O	O
P	N	P	P	A	P	A	O	D	O	N	Y	C	Y	S	R	D
R	R	A	B	M	G	L	R	L	I	O	N	G	R	I	D	E
E	E	R	S	E	O	O	O	N	O	I	A	A	A	C	Y	C
D	N	A	P	N	P	C	E	B	T	T	G	L	T	S	H	I
A	N	S	M	H	I	N	T	X	P	U	A	O	U	B	O	B
T	S	I	Y	R	O	Y	E	I	O	L	S	M	B	A	S	E
O	L	T	R	Z	H	Q	M	S	E	O	A	N	I	H	C	L
R	E	E	O	C	C	C	E	G	U	V	K	N	R	L	U	D
S	T	S	I	G	O	L	O	H	T	E	I	N	T	R	C	O
J	A	P	A	N	I	U	S	T	S	U	R	C	T	S	E	D

Word Search

1. The month in which the Earth environment day is celebrated: _____ *(June)*

2. The three R's of recycling are reduce, _____ and recycle. *(reuse)*

3. The layer in the stratosphere that protects the earth from the ultraviolet rays: _____ *(Ozone)*

4. The second Atom bomb explosion took place in this city: _____ *(Nagasaki)*

5. Kyoto protocol was signed in this country: _____ *(Japan)*

6. The most populated country in the world: _____ *(China)*

7. The elimination of a species of a living organism from the earth: _____ *(extinction)*

8. Illegal hunting of animals: _____ *(Poaching)*

9. A grassland ecosystem: _____ *(Savanna)*

10. Abbreviation of the United Nations Environmental Programme _____ *(UNEP)*

11. The first element of all food chains: _____ *(Plants)*

12. Parasites that live inside the host body:_____ *(Enteroparasites)*

13. Scientists who study the behaviour of wild animals: _____ *(Ethologists)*

14. Animals that live in the soil _____ *(Terricolous)*

15. Change in the hereditary characteristics displayed by successive generations of a species: _____ *(Evolution)*

16. Defence technique in which an animal changes its appearance/colour to blend with its surroundings: _____ *(Camouflage)*

17. Animals that prey on other animals: _____ *(Predators)*

18. The outermost layer of the earth's surface: _____ *(Crust)*

19. Decayed plant material used as fertilizer: _____ *(Compost)*

20. The element used to make microprocessor chips in computers: _____ *(Silicon)*

21. A small river or a stream flowing into a bigger river: _____ *(Tributary)*

22. Plants that grow in water: _____ *(hydrophytes)*

23. The person who started the Chipko Movement: _____ *(Bahuguna)*

24. The scientist who coined the term 'ecological succession': _____ *(Hult)*

25. A white alkaloid used for medicinal purposes _____ *(Quinine)*

26. Premature dropping of leaves due to air pollution: _____ *(Abscission)*

27. The unit used to measure sound: _____ *(Decibel)*

28. The minamata disease is caused by this element: _____ *(Mercury)*

29. Fog full of smoke: _____ *(Smog)*

30. Scientific study of the atmosphere: _____ *(Meteorology)*

31. Study of the movement, distribution and quality of water on earth: _____ *(Hydrology)*

32. Study of lakes: _____ *(Limnology)*

33. Scientific study of the climate: _____ *(Climatology)*

Word Search

Solution

june
reuse
ozone
nagasaki
japan
china
extinction
poaching
savanna
unep
plants
entroparasites
ethologists
terricolous
evolution
camouflage
predators
crust
compost
silicon
tributary
hydrophytes
bahuguna
hult
quinine
abscission
decibel
mercury
smog
meteorology
hydrology
limnology
climatology

CROSSWORD

Crossword

Down

2. The largest living mammal in the world (BLUE WHALE)
3. The process of placing a protective covering around plants to prevent evaporation of moisture (MULCHING)
4. The unit used to measure the frequency of sound (HERTZ)
6. The phenomenon of animal inactivity during hot and dry season (AESTIVATION)
7. The largest ocean (PACIFIC)
10. Organisms living in the lowest region of a body of water (BENTHOS)
11. The bird that lays the biggest eggs (OSTRICH)
13. The type of rock formed through the cooling of lava (IGNEOUS)
15. The first Earth summit was held in this country (BRAZIL)
17. The most active volcano located in Hawaii (KILAUEA)
18. Gigantic ocean waves caused by an earthquake or a volcanic eruption (TSUNAMI)
21. The act of changing in order to adjust to the changing surroundings (ADAPTATION)
22. A green pigment that enables green plants to prepare their own food (CHLOROPHYLL)
25. Organisms that only consume plants (HERBIVORES)

Across

1. The primary source of energy on the earth (SUN)
2. The process through which hydra reproduce (BUDDING)
3. It is also known as marsh gas (METHANE)
5. A type of fertile soil deposited by rivers and streams (ALLUVIAL)
8. The largest component of air (NITROGEN)
9. When these plates shift, earthquakes occur (TECTONIC)
12. The biggest and most populated continent in the world (ASIA)
14. A weather current that originates in eastern tropical Pacific Ocean (EL NINO)
16. He is also known as father of evolution (DARWIN)
19. A nest of crocodile eggs (CLUTCH)
20. The highest plateau, also called 'the roof of the world' (TIBETAN)
23. The layer of the atmosphere in which airplanes fly (STRATOSPHERE)
24. An organism that lives on another and causes it is harm (PARASITE)
26. Animals with backbones or spinal columns (VERTEBRATES)
27. Gigantic reptiles that lived in the Mesozoic Age and are now extinct (DINOSAURS)
28. These organisms have joined limbs and an external skeleton (ARTHROPODS)

Crossword

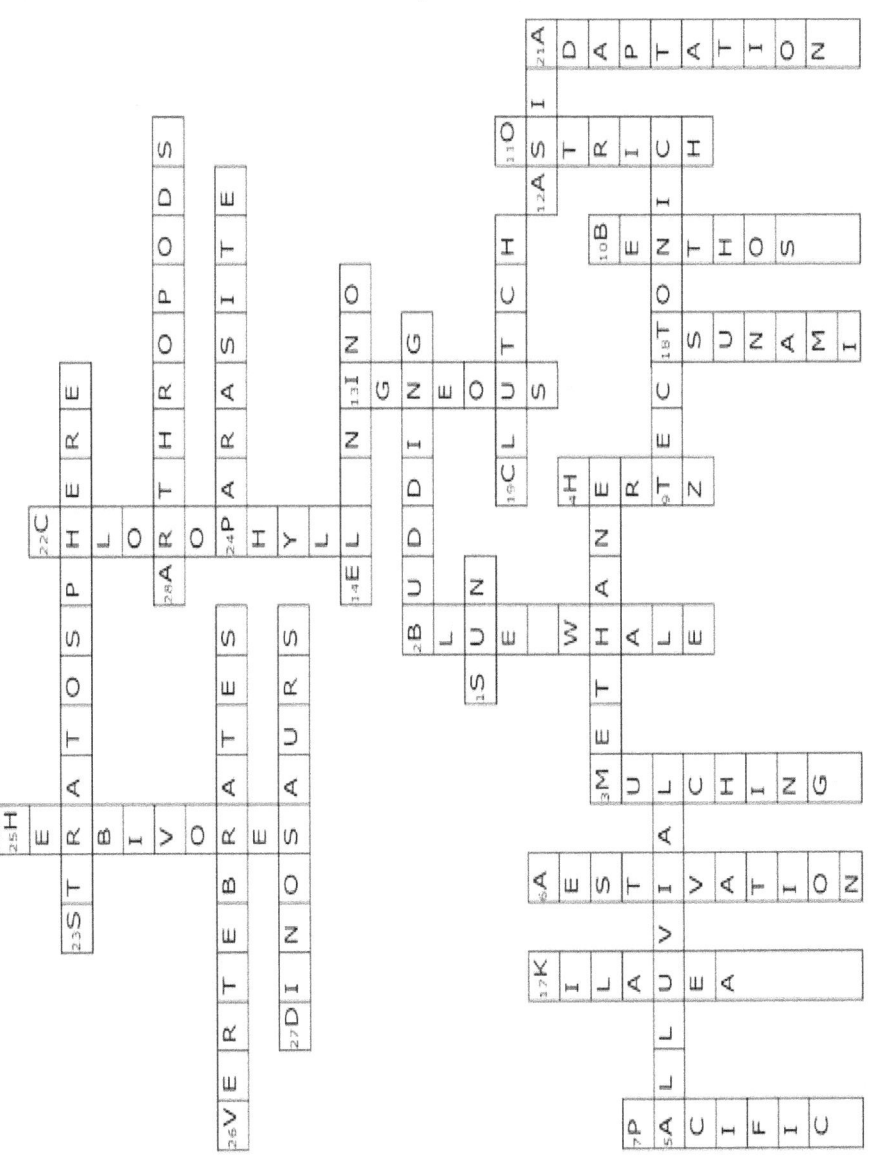